The Wishing World

The Wishing World

Todd Fahnestock

STARSCAPE

A TOM DOHERTY ASSOCIATES BOOK · NEW YORK

THE WISHING WORLD

Interior illustrations by Tricia Zimic

A Starscape Book
Published by Tom Doherty Associates, LLC
175 Fifth Avenue
New York, NY 10010

www.tor-forge.com

The Library of Congress Cataloging-in-Publication Data
is available upon request.

ISBN 978-0-7653-8588-8 (hardcover)
ISBN 978-0-7653-8590-1 (e-book)

Our books may be purchased in bulk for promotional, educational, or business use. Please contact your local bookseller or the Macmillan Corporate and Premium Sales Department at 1-800-221-7945, extension 5442, or by e-mail at MacmillanSpecialMarkets@macmillan.com.

First Edition: October 2016

Printed in the United States of America

0 9 8 7 6 5 4 3 2 1

To Elowyn
Your imagination makes the world a bigger place.
Keep that feather close.

To Dash
My favorite superhero. You are a mirror of justice
and strength for us all.

To Brighteyes
Your gaze upon me lights my way.

Acknowledgments

Like the Wishing World herself, this novel was created by the interweaving of many people's imaginations and talents. I am excited to acknowledge those who included their threads in this group-created story. A big thank-you to:

Elowyn Fahnestock: For making me write this book. Your imagination is boundless, and your sense of story and character humbles this old writer. Thank you for being the inspiration for Lorelei and for bringing countless *Wishing World* characters to life, like Ripple, Sir Real, and the Swisherswashers. And thanks for our walks in the park where we came up with the cool *Wishing World* movie posters.

Dashiell Fahnestock: Ferbleticks! Oofatruts! I can't wait to use them in the next *Wishing World* book. Thank you for your excitement for this story and for the adventure walks where we created *Wishing World* characters. A big thanks for Huggy-Bug the Pug! Most especially, thanks for being your heroic self so I could sketch you into the Mirror Man.

Lara Fahnestock: For telling me not to share the book with anyone outside our family until it was done. That created a magic I hadn't expected. For being my constant backboard for ideas. For being my every draft reader and my sanity-meter. None of this happens without you, my love.

Katie Bond and Amanda Rivera: For being such amazing champions of this story, and for letting me read the story to your second and fourth grade classes. The children's feedback was integral to shaping the final draft.

Callie Brown: For offering to help me publish *The Wishing World* with your allowance. I was (and still am) moved.

Aaron Brown: For reading the story to your children and letting me know just how close the book was to being done.

Bess Cozby: For being this story's champion at Tor, and

for being such an amazing editor. You've spoiled me. It is a joy to work with you. Every area I love, you highlight. Every area I silently question, you somehow find and give the perfect advice to help me shape and polish it to a bright shine. You're so talented, and I'm over the moon that this story gets to benefit from your expertise.

Alex Dailey: For knowing we had something with these characters before I even knew. When this story was just a few silly, slapped-together adventures told orally to children in the car as we drove to the hot springs in Carbondale, you turned a laser focus on me and said, "You should do something with that. The kids were captivated."

Megan Foss: For being my always fan and always friend. I keep writing because of you and those like you who can't wait for the next words.

Ellen Golliher: For being a great friend. Your enthusiasm for my writing cracked open the door to a bigger world. I'll never forget it.

Bill Golliher: For taking a chance on a little story. You took this from an excited conversation with Ellen to the big leagues. Thank you for being this book's champion.

Liana Holmberg: For being my early editor. For your unwavering belief in this story from the first moment you read it. You saw the diamond in the rough, and you were absolutely artful in bringing it into the light. Thank you for giving me no false praise so that when I heard the excitement in your voice when you said "You nailed it!" I knew the hard work had come to fruition. Thank you for everything. I cannot stress enough how you elevated this novel. You cultivated me, helped me evolve into the writer that this story needed.

Amelia Husbands: For your heartfelt joy after reading this story. And for presenting me with your handmade peanut butter cup and saying, "Thank you for writing my favorite book ever!" We'll see you in the *Wishing World*.

Chris Mandeville: For all of the wonderful feedback and encouragement for this story. Writing group partners to the end!

Tami Miller and Andrea Diaz del Valle: Thank you for being early readers. Your enthusiasm for the story spurred me on.

Emily Sherwood: You were there when the final piece clicked into place. I couldn't have made this story without you and the wonderful space you held for its creation.

Jim Swayze: For the many breakfasts. You helped me see what I needed to do and inspired me to do it. You helped this story fly. You have a knack for encouraging people to reach for the best inside themselves. Thank you for everything.

Carla Wirtz and Chris Lamson: For being Auntie Carrie and

Uncle Jone. I am so grateful for your ongoing support of this journey.

The Clanping Children: And finally, my thanks to all the children at Clanping who listened in rapt attention as the sun was going down and it was time to go to bed. This story was made for you and every other little person who holds the boundless potential of childhood.

The Wishing World

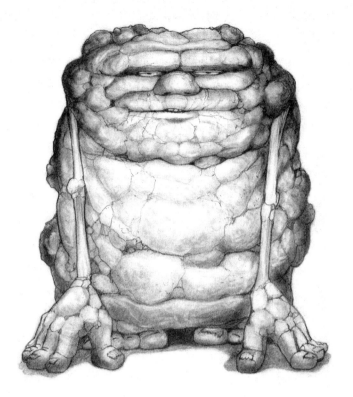

CHAPTER *I*

I RAN LIKE THERE WAS A MONSTER BEHIND ME. BECAUSE ONE
year ago today, there had been. Black tentacles slithered right out
of the rain and snatched my little brother. Snatched my parents,
too. That's the way it happened. Freaky truth, right? Bright like
a neon sign in your face.

Too bad nobody believed me.

The clouds were low and dark, bellies full of water, so I didn't
stop running until I got to my house. By then my legs were jelly.

Lungs burning. I had that metal taste in my mouth that you get when you run too hard. Florid Flecks of Phlegm. Gick.

The towering streetlight made a bright circle on the blacktop, the sidewalk, and the sloped lawn. The first rain droplets speckled my face lightly like they were innocent. Like they hadn't snatched my whole childhood away. But I was done being afraid. I was done flinching. I stood still with my fists clenched and let the drops hit me. I wanted my family back.

I spat out the nasty acid taste and tried the purple front door. Locked. And I didn't have a key anymore. Auntie Carrie and Uncle Jone had sold my house last week and sent me to a sleepover in the old neighborhood to make me feel better. Like *that* works. Have a pillow fight and a cup of hot chocolate, and you'll forget they're selling your house. You'll forget you ever had a brother or a mom or a dad. Welcome to the new normal. You get with the program yet, Lorelei?

No. Double no with a forget-you on top.

So I'd slipped past my best friend's parents. They thought I was tucked deep in my sleeping bag. Turns out five big stuffed animals look a lot like a Lorelei lump. But they would notice I was gone soon. They would check on me. Auntie Carrie and Uncle Jone would have asked them to. My aunt and uncle were trying to be "good parents," trying everything to make "the transition" easier on me. Auntie Carrie cried sometimes because I wouldn't respond to the nice things she did, wouldn't listen to her advice. They just didn't get it. I didn't need a replacement family; I didn't want a replacement family. I needed my brother and my mother and my father back. Nothing else even mattered. Nothing.

This last year I had been searching, doing everything I could to find my missing family. And wow, nobody liked that. Adults hate it when girls hitchhike, or go camping in the woods by themselves without telling anyone, or do Internet searches on kidnappers, then e-mail them questions.

When you do things like that, they use words like "trauma" and "delusions." They talk to you slowly, say everything twice, like you can't understand them the first time.

They used to call me imaginative, decisive. A good student and a better friend. But since the rain and the tentacles, since Narolev's Comet streaked the sky, it was Loopy Lorelei and her not-so-cute delusions. My replacement parents didn't know what to do with me, so they sent me to the creepy shrink, Mr. Schmindly.

Adults don't have a snappy solution for tentacles in the rain. Can we focus on the tentacles, adults?

No. Double no with a sit-down-and-be-quiet on top.

So I stopped pleading with them. Now my caring replacement family was afraid I was some kind of mute because I didn't cry anymore. But I stopped crying because it didn't do anything. Crying was really just waiting. Except with tears.

I was done waiting.

Dad said that life is like a story, and we get to fill it with what we want. Well, this last year of my story sucked, and I was going to rewrite it.

Then last week I got the Big Idea: Dad's comet stone. Dippy Lorelei. That was the first thing I should have thought of after the rainstorm. Narolev's Comet had been in the air when all the bad stuff happened; it was why we had been in the mountains in the first place. What if it was linked to what had happened? It had to be. Dad said he'd had a chunk of it in the basement, back in the crawl space. And the skeezoids who bought my house were moving in tomorrow. I couldn't wait one second longer.

I shook the thoughts away. I had to get going. My replacement family could be on their way right now. I looked up at the dark, overcast sky. I couldn't see Narolev's Comet, but it was up there somewhere, past those heavy clouds, streaking across the sky. I could feel it, looking down with its white eye.

I walked past the FOR SALE: SOLD sign stuck in my lawn, past the giant green bush to the backyard fence, and I thought of my brother Theron. He was always climbing this fence because the gate didn't work. He was always climbing everything.

Without Mom and Dad, I woke up most nights feeling like I was falling with no one to catch me. But without Theron, I felt like I'd lost my arm. Awake or asleep, I felt like I was missing something because he and I had almost always been together. The first memory of my life was when he was born. He showed up early. The midwife didn't get there in time. So I stood right there in the upstairs bathroom watching him take his first breath, squalling in a half-filled tub of water.

Theron was a protector. He fought that mean girl Shandra when she pushed me down and punched me. He leapt from the monkey bars and collared Danny Brogue when that bully stole my Halloween candy. Last year, he even stood between me and the fourth grade substitute teacher, Mrs. Coswell, when she blamed me for something Shandra had done. Theron threw a chair that time. He couldn't be still when something wasn't fair, or when someone he loved was threatened. He didn't know what else to do but fight.

And I protected him, too. Theron had nightmares every night. When he woke up thrashing and huffing like he'd run a mile, I would tell him good stories to calm him down. I would send him back to sleep and save him from the monsters in his head.

I jumped up, grabbed the top of the fence, and swung a leg over. It was up to me to find out where he had gone. Where they had all gone. Nothing else mattered.

I'm just like Theron, I thought. *Strong as a gorilla. I can do four pull-ups.*

I could really only do three. But imagining what I *couldn't* do never helped.

See it real, make it real. Do it real. One practice pull-up at a time.

I hoisted myself up, twisted, and balanced on top of the fence, letting my breath out.

I stretched, reached for the rain gutter, and caught it with my fingertips. Slowly, I pulled myself up. I hooked my heel into the rain gutter and leaned forward. It groaned, but I ignored it. It wasn't going to fall.

I rolled my body onto the sloped roof. Dark rain dots marked the shingles.

I am an Olympic gymnast, I thought, standing up. *I can balance on anything.*

I leaned into the roof and walked toward the upstairs window. Each step was tricky. My backpack was heavy, jammed with food instead of stuffed animals for the sleepover, and kept pulling me to the side . . . .

My foot slipped and I went down so fast I cried out. I hit the shingles and slid to the edge of the roof.

"No!" I shouted and jammed my heel into the rain gutter.

It clanged loudly and shook . . .

I drew a sharp breath, pushing hard on it, trying to get higher up as I stared at the drop below.

The gutter gave way with a sharp *crunk*.

Double suck with a yikes on top.

I shrieked and went over the edge, falling to the wood chips in the yard below.

CHAPTER *2*

At first, I thought I was dead, but if I was dead, I wouldn't have this need to breathe so badly.

You should be able to knock the wind back into yourself after you get the wind knocked out of you. Instead, it just feels like you're dying . . . dying . . . until . . .

I sucked in a great big breath.

Leapin' lungsuckers!

My backpack was jammed underneath me. Little drops raced

toward my face. I bit my lip and laid there, breathing hard, blinking away the stinging rain.

I'd just slid off a wet rooftop. And *that* was super smart. Maybe this whole thing was ridiculous. Maybe I should just lay here until they found me. And then Auntie Carrie would give me her worried face, her hands hovering near me like she wanted to touch me but was afraid she'd break me. And Uncle Jone would take me fishing again, take me somewhere quiet to spend "quality time." Don't talk about what's bothering her. Don't focus on that. She might start with the weird stories again. Just fish and try not to look at her.

I stood up and tears pricked my eyes.

The rain gutter had broken in the center and leaned like a ramp up to the corner of the house. I walked back to the old fence, hunched over, taking great big shuddering breaths. I was about to cry. Oh perfect.

I bit my lip, stared at the fence to make the tears stop, and then I saw the names.

Rocket-Boots Girl and Thorn Boy.

They were carved into the fence post. Theron and my superhero alter egos from when we were little, when he was four years old and I was six. We would race around the yard, creating stories where the heroes win and the bad guys lose. Always beating them. Always together. Good stories. Not stories where a girl's family disappears and she's all alone.

This story sucked. I needed a better one.

See it real. Make it real. Do it real.

I put my finger over the words and traced a new story over the superhero names. I wrote it slowly, carefully, like it was the only story that had ever mattered: *Lorelei climbed to the window. She crossed the roof without falling and went into her house.*

The wood seemed warmer where I had touched it. The rain seemed to shimmer, and I stopped. I balled up my fists and looked around. No tentacles launched out of the dark.

But I had felt something, and that gave me hope, like I was on the right track. Like I could feel Dad's comet stone somewhere in this house, and that it meant something. That it would explain the unknowable. All those things that the adults thought hadn't happened.

I jumped onto the fence. It rocked and I started up, hand over hand.

Don't think. Just do. I am a giant crab. I walk on slick rocks like they're sandpaper.

I rolled back onto the roof, started inching my way toward the window, careful of each step on the wet shingles.

Lightning flashed overhead. Thunder rumbled. Rain came down harder.

The window is right in front of me. I am already there.

I scooted, breathed, scooted some more. I slipped, then caught myself and held very still. I breathed there for a minute, then started forward again.

This is my story. A better story.

I looked only at the window. A little closer. A little closer . . .

Then I was there. I pushed it open, slipped inside, and fell to my knees. My wet hands slapped the hardwood floor.

I let the ache of the fall fill me now. I let it hurt. I was safe. This was home, where I belonged. Where my family belonged.

I got up and got straight to business. Dad's comet stone was the clue, my last hope. I'd tried everything else, so this had to work.

I went downstairs, squeezing through the thin, wooden-planked doorway into the spooky basement. All the junk my father had stored down there was gone. I climbed the shelves and slithered on my belly into the crawl space underneath the floors, flicking away spiders and searching with the little flashlight I'd brought. I peered into every dark, dirty corner, under every steel heater duct. The comet stone wasn't there. So I climbed back down and looked behind the furnace, through the crack in the brick wall that led underneath the bathroom. I checked everywhere. I checked everything.

Don't give up.

Clenching my teeth, I left the basement and went up to the main floor. I looked in the kitchen, the living room, the dining room. Every corner. Every closet. Every cupboard. Everywhere.

Dead end, Lorelei. Dead everything.

I stood in the center of the kitchen, clenching my fist.

I whirled around and went upstairs. There was no comet stone. Dad had made it up to amuse us. To entertain us. Like he did with so many things. Dorky Dad and his funny stories.

I stood in front of Mom and Dad's room, looking with eyes that saw back to when we lived here. I could feel them here, my family. I could see Theron running crazy through the bedroom, leaping onto the giant bed and body-slamming Dad. Then the wrestling would begin. Theron and I were always a team when we wrestled with Dad. It was the only way we could pin him.

I moved from Mom and Dad's bedroom into Theron's room. It was empty like everything else. There were no shelves filled with superhero action figures. No cutouts of Spider-Man, Captain America, and Black Panther on the wall. No basket of toy swords, bows, shields, and helmets.

Now only dust bunnies lived here, curled up in the corner around one stray Lego.

The rain outside streaked the window.

I touched the necklace Dad had given me in the mountains when we'd all gone camping to see the comet a year ago today. The necklace had a white stone in a little silver clasp. He'd also given Theron a silvery rock that looked like a knight. "From the comet," he had told us. Except they weren't real. His big piece of comet stone was a big fake, and I should have known that. I'd done the research. Bits of rock that fell to Earth were called meteorites. Comets were too far away to drop bits into our atmosphere.

I closed my eyes and that night came back in a rush.

"Stay here!" Mom said, looking back into the tent, which sagged with the weight of the water pouring onto it. "Stay here and I'll find them."

"Mom, don't go!"

"It'll be okay, sweetie. I'll be right back. I promise." Mom kissed me on the forehead and then she was gone.

Lightning flashed. Shadowy tentacles writhed over the tent. Menace oozed through the fabric. Tentacles were trying to get to me, trying to reach into the tent.

"Mom!" I screamed, clenching Dad's necklace in my fist. It felt hot, like it had a fire inside it.

The tent lit up and thunder boomed like lightning had struck the ground right outside. The shadow tentacles suddenly vanished and a different shadow took their place, dark and tall, painted on the side of the tent. I shrieked.

The shadow had a huge head, round and sloped into a beak-like muzzle, and four legs like a dog. Its back was deformed, with bumps behind its shoulders. I screamed again, but the creature didn't try to come inside. It just stood there in the flashes of light as rain lashed the tent.

"Theron!" I called, but no one answered.

The beak-nosed dog-thing remained there throughout the storm. I didn't dare go outside. I waited until morning. When sunlight filtered through the clouds and the rain stopped, the shadow was gone. So was my family.

I pulled the "comet stone" necklace out from underneath my wet shirt and sat down cross-legged, wriggled my left arm out of my backpack, and let it thump on the floor. I took a shuddering breath and calmed myself. I wanted a "Lorelei sandwich," when Mom and Dad hugged me at the same time. "And I'm the jelly in the middle," I would say, squeezing them so tight.

I wanted Theron back, to walk with me through all the scary things. To make the good stories with me again. "I'll be Thorn Boy, and you be Rocket-Boots Girl. Grab my hand and let's fly, Rocket-Boots Girl!"

They had taken away his bed, of course, but I imagined it. In my mind, I put back the quilt Granny had made for him: dark blues, light blues, and whites. Granny had cleverly sewn together triangle scraps to make circle patterns, and they had wondrous pictures on them: shooting stars and colorful toucans, a pug dog and a silver tree, flying foxes and tall flowers, griffons and sharks.

And there was clutter in the corner, of course. Theron's stack of comic books and clothes and half-assembled Legos, all in a pile.

I tried to believe the story. Couldn't I just live there instead, with my family a year and a day ago? But Dad's big comet stone wasn't here. It wasn't my clue. I was back to where I started. Back to nothing and no clues and no family and they'd sold my house to some skeezoids I'd never met. My story was weak. It peeled away like wallpaper.

A thin whimper leaked out of my mouth. I cleared my throat and hit my fist on the hardwood floor and made it stop.

I drew a deep breath, stood up, and held out my hand.

I'll find you. I wrote the words on the air. *I will find you.*

I squinched my eyes and imagined the words staying, like they were written in fire, hovering and flickering. Like they were *truth*.

Lightning flashed, and my necklace suddenly felt hot like that night in the rain. Thunder boomed, and an enormous shadow appeared, slanted across the ceiling: the same shadow from outside my tent a year ago.

I screamed and spun around, stepped backward, tripped on my pack, and sprawled on the floor. Nice moves, Grace.

A creature crouched in the doorway to Mom and Dad's room, ready to spring. His front claws clutched the hardwood floors, thin points digging into wood. His giant eagle head swiveled, taking in the room at a glance. Wings flexed, bumped the doorjamb, then pressed tightly against his sides, the flanks of a golden lion.

The beast focused his fierce gaze on me. He looked powerful

enough to break a hole through the ceiling. A lion and a giant eagle mixed together. A griffon! Larger than a horse and moving and *real*!

"Doolivanti," the griffon said in a deep voice, and he bowed his head.

CHAPTER *3*

I T TALKED! I OPENED MY MOUTH TO SAY SOMETHING, BUT what do you say to a talking griffon that appears in your house?

He stepped toward me, and I scrambled backward until my back hit the wall.

But then he tripped. One of his talons had sunk too deeply in the wood and didn't pull free. He crashed forward, beak smacking the floor. Wood splintered as he surged back upright and yanked his talon free. There was so little room for his huge body that his lion butt crashed into the doorjamb, cracking it.

"Jeepers," I whispered.

He shook his eagle head. His ruffled feathers laid perfectly flat, and he stood up straight, lifted his head high. He looked like a cat when it does something dorky: *you didn't see that. That didn't happen.*

I laughed, then clapped a hand over my mouth.

He cleared his throat. "I cannot linger," he said, beak held high. "You must send me back."

"Send you back?"

"You are the Doolivanti from the fabric house," the griffon rumbled. "Yes?"

Fabric house? It meant the tent! The rainstorm!

"My friends are in danger, Doolivanti, and I must protect them."

I blinked once, long and meaningfully. He was so big and real and . . . big! I pinched my arm so hard my eyes watered. He didn't go away.

All right, I thought. I'd spent the last year trying to convince the adults of something utterly weird. Now weird was in my face. Talking. And I was going to get some answers. I stood up and took a tiny step forward.

"Did you eat my parents?" I blurted.

"I do not eat people." The griffon snorted, then focused his eagle gaze on me. "I cannot talk right now. You must send me back. My friends—"

"You think *I* brought you?" I said.

"You brought me here with your magic, of course," he stated, as though this was irrefutable fact. "You are a Doolivanti."

"I-I was writing on the air. I wrote . . . a better story. What

I want it to be. I want to find my brother. My mom and dad. I wasn't doing magic."

The griffon cocked his giant head to the side, and his fierce tone softened. "You lost your family the night of the storm. To the Ink King."

"To the who? The ink thing?" I clenched my fists and made myself say the next words. "Did you take them? Were those your tentacles?"

"I have no tentacles!" The griffon's wings flexed, knocking into the doorjamb as if he would shake the thought away. "Only the Ink King slithers in the dark like a coward. That was the night he stole the Eternal Sea from the sea princess. It was he who took your parents. He came for you next, but that I could not abide. He is a thief and a villain, and I would not let him hurt you."

"You saved me?" I asked, and my heart rose a little. He had been guarding me that night, not threatening me. "Thank you," I said softly.

The griffon cleared his throat uncomfortably. "Well. It was the only thing to do." He bowed his head. When he straightened, he said, "Please forgive me, Doolivanti. In my haste, I have abandoned my manners. I am Gruffilandimus the Griffon, and I am pleased to meet you."

"Gruffilandimus?"

He hesitated a moment like he was going to admit to something. But then he didn't. He said, "Yes."

I took a step toward him, reached out, and touched his beak. It was hard as steel, and warm.

"Please, Doolivanti," he said, and his beak vibrated under my hand. I yanked it away.

Todd Fahnestock

"Doolivanti. You keep saying that. What is that?"

"A traveler. A wish maker," the griffon said. He made a click-ing sound with his beak. "You were wishing for something you wanted very much, and you called out to Veloran."

"What do you mean? Who's Veloran?"

"The land where I live. Veloran loves those who dream."

"So you're saying I made you come here because I wrote the story I wanted?" I asked.

"Of course."

"Of course?" I didn't get how that was an "of course." "Okay," I said. "Why you? Why not just give me my family?"

"Am I to know this?" he said.

"Uh, if not you, then who?"

"Please, Doolivanti. We are attempting to free the princess from the Ink King, and the grimrock that guards her has at-tacked my friends." The griffon crouched. "I must save them." His wings opened in impatience, hit the doorjamb again, then closed.

"What's a grimrock?" I asked.

"Please, Doolivanti! I am out of time!"

My mind spun. Could I really be the reason why he was standing here in front of me? Had I made him come by writing what I wanted?

I raised my finger and wrote on the air: *the griffon scratched his nose.*

The griffon twitched, bumping his beak against the door-jamb.

I blinked. No way.

I shook my head. Okay okay. That could have been an acci-dent. He'd been crashing into things since he showed up.

I wrote on the air again: *the griffon told a joke.*

The griffon looked down at me, and a little curve appeared at the corner of his beak. "When my friend Pip the toucan first met my friend Squeak the mouse, he said, 'Cheesed to meet you.'"

The griffon snapped his beak shut and looked confused.

Flippin' flyin' frogs! I mean, that was the worst joke in the history of jokes. But it *was* a joke!

"Okay!" I said. "I'll do it." I raised my hand and wrote words on the air: *the griffon went home.*

It grew darker. The comet throbbed at my throat.

I sucked in a breath and looked all around. I raised my hand and wrote again: *the griffon found his friends. He—*

Orange light flickered against the wall.

"More," the griffon encouraged.

The griffon flew back to his friends and saved them from the grimrock.

Orange-lit sandstone blocks appeared behind the white paper-board of Theron's bedroom wall. They were huge and perfectly square, and there was no sky there, just a dark ceiling. It was a kind of hallway, like a crypt under a pyramid. Egyptian-ish. I thought I saw something blue flap past. A bat? The whole thing was like a movie with fuzzy edges. The griffon reached out a claw, but it *thunked* against the wall. He looked back at me.

I wrote: *the griffon went home.*

A sharp heat rose in my chest. "Ow!" I pressed a hand into it.

The griffon reached out again, and this time his claw flattened and bent sideways, like it had become part of the movie.

"Well done, Doolivanti!" he shouted, and leapt into the picture. Then, like a watercolor in the rain, the image wavered and began to slide down the wall in streaks.

. . . The Ink King . . . he is a thief and a villain. It was he who took your parents.

And the Ink King came from Veloran, too.

My scalp felt prickly, and my heart beat so fast it hurt.

I lurched across the room, yanking my pack behind me. Sweeping my "pencil," I wrote as fast as I could.

Lorelei followed the griffon. She found her family.

I jumped into the painting.

CHAPTER 4

THE GRIFFON SAILED EFFORTLESSLY INTO THE PAINTING,
landed on the loose sand floor in the corridor, wings flaring. A
torch in a metal bracket on the wall flickered from his gust of
wind.

But when I jumped after him, a thin film caught me, like
plastic wrap had been stretched over the movie in the wall.

I heard a voice in my mind, whispering, and my imagination
went wild. Now it's not like my imagination hasn't ever gone
wild before. But this was like a movie trailer with a bunch of

flashing scenes, like someone had pushed "play" in my brain and was looking at all the awesome things I'd ever done in my life and all the stuff I'd ever dreamed of doing. It showed times I'd played with my friends, with Theron. It showed me every book I'd ever read, every movie I'd ever watched, everything I ever thought, all in an instant.

I know, right? Swallow that. Jeepers! It was like guzzling a giant orange Fanta, fifty gallons at once. Yum? Maybe?

Loremaster . . . the voice whispered, and the name was perfect. My heart, squeezed with the loss of Theron and Mom and Dad, suddenly felt light. I was calm and certain, not scared. Not lost. I could see happiness like sunlight right in front of me. *This* was the name I'd been searching for. My real name. The name I'd secretly always wanted everyone to call me.

Threads of silver and blue, my two favorite colors, flew out of nowhere, and started lacing themselves around me. They wove and fitted together as fast as a thought, sewing new clothes. Black leggings with silver boots. A long-sleeved blue jacket with silver embroidery and little designs on the cuffs, buttoned in the front with discs of silver. It was elegant and awesome, the clothes I would have chosen if I could have made up exactly what I wanted. A satchel filled with paper and quills for writing formed at my side. I could see myself standing on a balcony and talking to a crowd in this, see myself riding a horse in this. I could do anything.

You are beloved. You are needed. A leader like no other . . . the voice whispered.

A light breeze twirled me and I floated in the air. I looked down at myself. *Loremaster.* The one who writes her own story, who changes the world around her, who could do anything, find anything. This was me; the me I could someday be, except I *was* her right here and right now when I needed her the most. I had no worries. Everything I envisioned would happen. There was nothing beyond my abilities—

"Stop!" I shouted. And I almost couldn't. I almost didn't. Another second and I wouldn't have.

I grabbed the beautiful fabric and pulled at it. It ripped at the top.

"I'm Lorelei!" I shouted, and my heart hurt. The loss of my family came flooding in again like a dam had broken inside me. Lorelei was lost and alone and had no friends she could talk to. Loremaster knew what to do. She knew who to ask and those she asked would follow her. Loremaster had as many friends as she wanted. And she knew how to find her parents. I could be Loremaster, that amazing ruler, thinker, doer. She knew how to make the hard choices. I wanted to be her so badly.

But some strange voice had jumped into my brain, taken my best memories, and turned me into something else. Spooky much? Double brainwashing with a zombie on top.

I yanked at the jacket, and it ripped. The whole outfit separated down the middle as though it had somehow been all one piece. Underneath, my T-shirt appeared, and my jeans. It felt like I was tearing my own skin, and I shouted. My heart burned, and I fell onto my hands and knees on the sandy floor in the Egyptian hallway. Theron's bedroom became flat behind me. It was now the painting, sliding slowly down the yellow block wall.

The outfit lay in pieces on either side of me, shimmered, and began to fade. I looked down at my chest, expecting to see my T-shirt torn, to see a scrape or a burn or something.

Instead, a little thread of fire fell out of my chest and hovered between my arms. The pain faded. It was as though the burn inside me had become that thread. It floated past my nose and up to the dark ceiling, then disappeared.

"What happened? What happened?" A blue toucan squawked right above me.

"Squeak!" To my left, a charcoal-gray mouse stood on its hind legs, looking at me. Its whiskers twitched.

A moan rose behind me. I spun around and saw an enormous, lumpy creature molded from gray rock. It hunched forward, a wide mouth opening in its head. Two long, thin arms hung down from blocky shoulders. It had thick elbows and huge hands.

That, my numb brain told me, *must be a grimrock.*

I looked to see if I could jump back into my house, but the painting was gone. There was only flickering torchlight on Egyptian walls.

I sucked in a breath to scream, but bit down on my tongue. *No! No screaming!*

The griffon leapt between me and the rock creature. His sliding claws threw a fan of sand into the air.

"You vanished. You vanished," the toucan squawked. "And now there's a girl? There's a girl?"

The stone creature roared, shuffling forward. "Not be here!"

"He means us! He means us!" the toucan squawked, flapping back so fast it smacked into the wall.

The griffon's talons scraped stone underneath the loose sand,

and he screeched so loudly it echoed through the tunnel. The torches flickered.

The grimrock slammed a fist into the floor, sending up a spray of sand, and rose to his full height. His head nearly touched the tall ceiling.

"We run. We run," the toucan said.

"We came to rescue the Princess of the Eternal Sea," the griffon said. "We will not run."

"You're not a hero, Gruffy! You're not a hero!"

"Gruffilandimus!" the griffon insisted.

"Gruffy!" the toucan repeated. "Gruffy!"

The grimrock swung again, but the griffon leapt upward. The strike whooshed underneath him, bashing into the wall in front of me. I staggered away, protecting my face from flying chips of rock. They stung my forearms like wasps. I gasped and looked down at the pinpricks of blood.

"We cannot beat it. Cannot beat it," the toucan squawked. "We should die so you can pretend? So you can pretend?"

"I do not pretend," the griffon said. He flapped up, pecked at the grimrock's head, and leapt over him. It sounded like an axe striking stone. "The princess is the key to overthrowing the Ink King."

"Waitaminute," I said. "This princess can overthrow the Ink King? The Ink King that stole my parents?"

"Squeak!" replied the mouse, as if he had answered my question. I took it as a yes.

"And she can beat the Ink King?" I asked.

"She is our only hope," the griffon said, landing on the other side of the grimrock.

I stepped forward to ask where the princess was, and how far the Eternal Sea was from here, and I totally forgot that there was a giant rock man right in front of me.

I got reminded really quick.

"You no come here!" The grimrock moaned, reaching for me. His coal-black eyes looked hurt and haunted, and a noise rumbled in his belly, distant and getting closer like an avalanche. I gaped up at him, and for some crazy reason, I thought of Theron.

The griffon leapt onto the grimrock's back. Rock popped as he dug in his talons, and the grimrock roared again, arching away from me and missing his grab.

"Wait!" I shouted. Theron became a total brat when he missed a meal. That wasn't an avalanche in the grimrock's belly. It was—

"Wait! Stop!" I shouted.

"Stop?" The griffon paused, his head reared back to deliver a sharp peck.

"What do you mean, 'stop'? What do you mean, 'stop'?" The toucan squawked.

"He's hungry!"

"And we're lunch! We're lunch!"

I grabbed my fallen backpack. I unzipped it and plunged my hand in, yanked out the peanut butter and jelly sandwiches.

The grimrock grasped at the griffon, but he leapt away. I ran up, standing right in front of the creature. He opened his enormous hand and reached down to crush me.

"Here!" I thrust the sandwiches up at him, smooshed together in my shaking fist. "Eat!" I yelled.

A deep crease folded the grimrock's forehead over his dark eyes. He stared, his hand hovering over me.

"You have food?" the grimrock asked. His voice sounded like someone calling up from the bottom of a well.

"For you!" I shouted.

"Th-th . . ." the grimrock stuttered. He balled up his fist and slammed it down beside me, shaking the ground and making the sand jump. The griffon screeched and launched into the air.

"Thank you!" The grimrock crashed to his knees. His fingers, each as long as my arm and twice as thick, opened to take the tiny sandwiches. I put them on his palm, and he tossed them into his mouth.

"Nice girl," the grimrock said. His frightening smile showed flat, stone teeth with gaps in between. He looked at my backpack. "You have more?"

"Squeak!" the mouse said.

"Right," the griffon replied, and he flew up the hallway, out of sight.

"I can't believe it. I can't believe it," the toucan squawked.

"I do have more." I rummaged around in my pack. I had two bananas, an apple, and half a box of Leapin' Lemurs cereal in a ziplock bag. I put them all into the grimrock's palm, and he threw them into his mouth without peeling the bananas or opening the bag. He didn't seem to notice the plastic in his meal.

He smiled. His stomach rumbled again. The rumble moved up his belly through his chest to his neck, and then the grimrock let out a thunderous burp. A breeze blew over me, smelling of wet earth after a long rain. I put my hand over my nose.

"You have more?" the grimrock asked.

"Um." I reached around my mother's steel water bottle and felt for anything else. All I found was a penny, a dime, and a lint-covered raisin.

I held up the raisin and shrugged. "You want this?"

The grimrock kept his wide mouth open. I tossed the raisin in and he ate it.

"More?" he asked.

"I, uh, I don't have any more," I said.

The grimrock's smile fell, and a worried look came into his coal eyes. "No more?"

"Oh no. Oh no," the toucan said, but just then, the griffon swooped back into the room carrying a bulging sheet, the corners clamped in his beak. He looked like a stork delivering a giant baby.

He dropped the sheet onto the floor and it burst open, spilling dozens of loaves of bread across the stones.

"Ahhhhh!" the grimrock said, sitting down with a *thoom*. He began grabbing fistfuls of the loaves and stuffing them into his mouth.

"Well played, Doolivanti," the griffon said, his talons clicking on the stones as he walked up to me and bowed.

"Squeak," said the mouse.

The griffon nodded. "Yes, of course. My apologies." He inclined his head. "These are my friends."

"I'm Pip. I'm Pip," said the toucan.

"Squeak!" said the mouse.

I looked at Pip and the griffon. "Is he saying something?"

"Can you not understand him?" Gruffy asked.

"Just squeaks."

"Well, allow me to introduce our most clever friend, Squeak."

"Squeak!" said Squeak.

"And you're Gruffilandimus?" I asked. "Or Gruffy?"

"Gruffilandimus," the griffon said quickly. He straightened and his chest broadened.

"Squeak-squeak-squeak," said Squeak softly, his whiskers twitching behind one of his paws. It sounded like he was laughing.

"His name is Gruffy. His name is Gruffy," Pip said.

"That *was* my name. I am now—"

"A new name doesn't make you braver. Doesn't make you braver," Pip squawked.

I put a hand on the griffon's feathery neck. "You're the bravest creature I've ever met. You don't need a long name to prove that." I said. "Gruffy is better."

The griffon paused, beak open. He looked down at me. His fierce gaze softened, and that curve appeared at the corner of his beak. "Very well, Doolivanti. I am Gruffy the griffon."

"You should stick around. Stick around," Pip said. "He never listens to anyone. Never listens to anyone."

"Well, I—"

"What is your name, Doolivanti? Your name, Doolivanti?" Pip asked.

"I am Lorelei," I said.

"Squeak," Squeak said.

"Not Rock Tamer? Rock Tamer? Or Sandwich Slinger? Sandwich Slinger?" Pip squawked.

"What are you talking about?" I asked. *Loremaster* . . . the whispering voice was like a quiet, receding echo. I ignored it.

"Squeak."

"Lorelei doesn't sound like any Doolivanti that I've ever heard of. That I've ever heard of," Pip said.

"Why not?" I asked.

"It is because she is better than all other Doolivantis," Gruffy interrupted.

His towering confidence in me made me feel hot in the face. "I don't, um . . ."

"Her family was stolen by the Ink King, even as the Eternal Sea was stolen from the princess. We shall restore them both."

"Yes," I said. "Yes, but . . ." I paused. Everything had happened so fast. Going to my old house, then rain and lightning, then falling off the roof. Then griffons and grimrocks and . . . My mind felt like a balloon with too much air, stretched to the limit, and how could I be sure the Ink King had my family? I wanted to believe it so badly . . .

"Are you sure the Ink King is the one who took my family?" I asked.

"Of course I am," Gruffy said.

"Of course he's not. Of course he's not. Any more than he's sure the princess is here. The princess is here."

The grimrock finished the bread, then leaned back against the wall, which shook, rock dust sifting down from the ceiling. His eyes slid shut.

"Full," he rumbled.

"I am certain the princess is here," Gruffy said. "Why else would there be a grimrock underneath the streets of Azure City?"

"Oh right. Oh right. You know it deep in your hero's bones. Your hero's bones."

Gruffy's wings flexed, as though he might leap into the air again. Pip flew backward, out of range.

"She's not even your princess! Not your—!" Pip started, but he was interrupted by the grimrock, who sat up and spoke.

"Princess?" he said, and his tiny eyes narrowed. "No can have princess."

CHAPTER 5

THE GRIMROCK STOOD UP ONE SHOULDER AT A TIME, RISING to its intimidating height. "Princess stay here," he said.

"You see?" Gruffy said as he swiveled to face the creature. "She is here."

"And now we're lunch again. We're lunch again," Pip replied.

The grimrock shook his head, and it sounded like grinding rocks. "Ink King return. Ink King punish Urath," he rumbled ominously. "Make Urath starve."

Gruffy bristled and crouched. One of his wings flared out, gently sweeping me behind him.

"Wait!" I shouted, my feet scraping against the rock floor. "Wait a minute! Stop fighting for a second." I tried to think. This was all so crazy and, at the same time, exactly what I'd asked for. A chance, just one chance, to find my family again. And here it was, if I could just believe it. My mind was spinning, and I had to sort it out. So I backed up and tried to stick to what I knew. I had come looking for clues. A magical griffon told me that a magical Ink King had taken my family to this place, called Veloran, through a sliding painting in the wall. Which was impossible, of course. I could almost believe I was dreaming except that my arms still stung from where rock chips had hit me. Except that I'd smelled the earthy yick of a grimrock's burp. Not to mention . . .

I paused to glance up at the talking toucan, the enormous griffon and the enormous-er grimrock, all watching me expectantly. I blinked hard and tried to make them go away like I'd done with Gruffy back in my house.

It didn't work. I glanced down at Squeak.

"Squeak," Squeak said, shrugging and raising his paws palm up.

So they were real. Double real with a mouse on top.

Unless I was in that "delusion" Mr. Schmindly talked about, and I was actually drooling on the floor of my house right now, this was happening. For really real.

This was my chance. What I'd asked for. Except I didn't know anything about where I was. I needed these creatures' help to find my family and bring them back.

"Okay," I said, "I'm going to sum up." I pointed at the grim-rock. "You. Urath. The Ink King keeps you here?"

"Urath cannot leave."

"Then the Ink King's a doofus. And he's made an enemy of everybody here," I said, looking at each of them in turn. "We should fight him together."

"We should? We should?" Pip squawked. "Fight the Ink King? Fight the Ink King?"

"Indubitably," Gruffy said.

"But he's the most powerful Doolivanti in Veloran! In Veloran!" Pip squawked. "He—"

"Not anymore," Gruffy said.

Pip rolled his eyes. "Okay, I like her, too. I like her, too. But that's more reason to—"

"Squeak," interrupted Squeak.

Gruffy smiled. "You see?" he said to Pip.

Pip flapped back and forth, agitated. "How do I get talked into this? How do I get talked into this?"

"Because you are a good friend," Gruffy said.

"So are we agreed?" I asked, watching Pip. He didn't seem convinced. I also wished I could understand the mouse. Everybody else seemed to. Pip didn't say anything else, so I continued. "The Ink King is a doofus, and somebody should smack him upside his inky head."

"Yes," said Gruffy.

"Squeak," said Squeak.

"Even I know that. Even I know that," Pip said.

"Then we work together," I said. I turned to the grimrock.

"We'll get you out," I said. "We'll get you away from the Ink King."

"Wait! Wait! Free the grimrock? Free the grimrock?" Pip flapped erratically overhead.

"Urath no can leave. Ink King make wall. Urath stay to starve."

"No!" I said. "You take us to the princess. We will find a way to get you out of here."

Urath rose up, his rocky head brushing the top of the tunnel. "Take Urath out?"

I waved away the dust that sifted down and coughed. "I promise." I turned to Gruffy, Pip, and Squeak. "Do we promise?"

"You don't free grimrocks, you cage 'em. You cage 'em," Pip squawked.

"Doolivanti," Gruffy said. "Grimrocks are dangerous. We cannot just let him loose on Azure City."

"The Ink King stole my family," I said. "And he stole this poor creature's freedom. We can't just let him do that!"

"That's not a poor creature. Not a poor creature," Pip squawked.

Gruffy looked hesitantly at the grimrock.

From behind them all came a quiet "squeak." Pip and Gruffy turned, and we all looked down at the tiny charcoal mouse.

"That is true," Gruffy said, "A creature in need is a creature in need."

He got all that from just one little squeak? Sheesh.

"But a grimrock—"

"Squeak squeak," Squeak interrupted Gruffy.

"Well you've all gone crazy. You've all gone crazy," Pip squawked.

"Squeak!"

"No, Pip. Our valiant friend speaks aright," Gruffy said, though he, too, sounded reluctant. He turned back to Urath. "Very well, grimrock—"

"Urath," I corrected him. Gruffy's huge eye swiveled to glance sidelong at me, and I thought there was a smile at the corner of his beak.

"Very well, Urath." Gruffy looked back at the grimrock. "If you assist us in freeing the princess, we shall make sure you are free of the Ink King."

Urath's little coal-black eyes became very wide. "Th-th . . ." He slammed his fist alarmingly onto the stone floor. I jumped and Pip flapped backward.

"Thank you," the grimrock finished.

CHAPTER *6*

"Princess down." Urath turned and headed into the
dark tunnel. We all followed. Soon, there were no torches in the
wall. The tunnel reminded me of the drainage pipe underneath
St. Michael's Street in the arroyo near Granny and Pop Pop's
house. Pitch black. I could barely see the outline of the griffon
next to me. I reached out and put a hand on Gruffy's feathery
ruff to steady myself. He seemed to be able to see just fine.

At least now we were getting somewhere, though. Less fighting. More doing. Except I had a million questions. Who was the

Ink King? Why would he steal my family? And if the princess was imprisoned during the same storm, as Gruffy seemed to think, did she have anything to do with my missing family?

"Why did the Ink King take the Eternal Sea from the princess?" I asked Gruffy.

"Who can say why villains do what they do?" Gruffy replied.

I frowned. That wasn't an answer. "Well, I want to know why he took my family. Maybe they're related."

"Indeed," Gruffy said. "Let us pose this question to him when we have brought him to his knees."

"Um, yes. But isn't there any way to know—"

Loreliar . . . a voice whispered. This one was completely different than the first whisper. It felt like someone was trying to pour oil in my ear.

I shook my head and turned around, peering into the absolute black behind us.

"Doolivanti?" Gruffy asked. "Are you well?"

"Did you hear that?" I asked.

The griffon peered up the hallway, then at me. "I heard nothing, Doolivanti. Does something follow us?"

"No. I thought I—"

Ahead in the tunnel, Urath said, "Princess here," and stopped.

I waited a long moment for the whisper to return, but it didn't. I gave one last glance up the dark hallway, then turned and jogged up to the bulky shadow of the grimrock.

There was a straight, faintly glowing blue line where the wall met the floor: light leaking underneath a door. I knelt down and put my fingers by the blue glow.

The door was made of thick wooden planks bound with iron.

An iron lock the size of my head was just below the curved iron handle.

"What's this glow?" I asked.

"Princess," Urath rumbled.

"The princess is glowing?" I asked.

"Open the door," Gruffy said to Urath.

"No key," he replied.

Gruffy put his talons over the giant handle and pushed. His feathers rippled, wings flexing, and the muscles in his lion legs bunched, but he finally let out a breath and shook his head.

He turned to Urath. "Can you bash it down?"

The giant swayed back and forth. His stomach rumbled like he was hungry again.

"This bad idea," Urath said. "Cannot get princess. Cannot stop Ink King."

"No." I put my hands on the grimrock's forearm, and it felt like the cold stones by the stream where we had camped in San Isabel. "It's a good idea. Do you want to be his prisoner forever?"

"Ink King leave Urath to starve." The grimrock shook his tiny head, making a sound like rocks scraping together. His hands slowly balled into fists.

"Urath, no!" I yelled.

Gruffy let out a screech, feathers standing up on his back.

A loud grinding and a metal *kronk* stopped us, and we looked back at the door.

Squeak emerged from the enormous keyhole of the lock. He was breathing hard, and he dropped the piece of wire he'd been holding and shook out his little paws. He looked at me and Gruffy in turn, then nodded.

"Squeak!" He jumped to the floor.

Urath stood there, his fists still balled up, but he didn't swing.

"See?" I said. "We got this door open. We'll get you out, too, okay?"

Urath didn't say anything, but he unballed his fists.

Gruffy pushed hard on the handle. It gave way with a rusty groan, and the door swung open, filling the hallway with blue light.

A girl with light blue skin lay sleeping on a stone bed, which rose up from the floor like the rest of the room had been carved away from it. She didn't move, despite the racket we had caused in the hallway. Was she in some kind of magical sleep?

Her arms were crossed over her chest, and her hair looked like a dark blue river with sparkles of light in it. Her dress looked like someone had poured blue paint over her and . . . it just stopped that way. It covered her entire body except for her webbed blue feet.

This was the girl who had lost her kingdom to the Ink King the same night I'd lost my family. It made us sisters, bound together by the doofus deeds of a bully.

Well, we were going to fix that.

CHAPTER 7

THE PRINCESS'S NOSE WAS STRAIGHT, ALMOST POINTED. HER
face was long, her chin sharp, and her closed eyes were slanted
upward. Her arm was cool to the touch.

Her eyelids fluttered, and I jumped back.

The princess sat upright and opened her eyes, which were all
blue with no whites. Um . . . weird much? I tore my gaze away
and saw a wound on her side, it glowed beneath the blue dress
like it was burning. It was small, and it looked just like the fiery

thread that had fallen out of my chest when I first came here. She caught my glance and put her hand over the wound.

"What is that?" I asked. I suddenly had a sinking feeling that I had hurt this elegant princess somehow, that there was a connection between that burn in my chest and that wound on her side. "Are you all right?"

But when the princess moved her hand, the fiery cut was gone.

"Thou'rt kind to ask." She dangled her feet over the edge of the stone bed. "'Tis true I am assailed by weakness. Prithee, to whence have I come?"

My parents had taken me to see Shakespeare in the Park once, and this princess sounded like those actresses.

"Azure City, your highness," Gruffy answered, bowing his head. "We have come to free you. This is the Doolivanti Lorelei, and our companions Pip and Squeak. Outside the door is Urath, the grimrock. Once your jailor, now he aids us in freeing you."

The princess blinked, as if trying to take all of that in after just waking up. I sure knew a lot about how that felt.

"I know not this city," the princess said. "'Tis one of the land kingdoms?"

"A human city, of the Triad," Gruffy said.

"The Triad . . . Thou dost speak of the desert. 'Twould account for my weakness." She pushed off the table, but couldn't bear her own weight and crumpled.

I caught her, put my hand around her waist, and brought her upright. She was as light as a leaf.

"Thou dost assist me and I know thee not. In my weakened state, there are many who would seize upon the chance to malign me."

"Malign you?" I was having a hard time understanding what she meant; her speech was so strange.

"To harm me. Some do such simply because they can, or because they crave that which belongs to another, or simply because they are nefarious at heart." She paused, staring at me through her dark blue lashes as if she was waiting for an answer to that. If that little thread of fire had gone out of me and into her, was she asking me if I'd done it on purpose?

"Well I'm not like that," I said, trying to remember what "nefarious" meant. I was pretty sure it wasn't anything good. "I'm not nefarious."

The princess paused. "I see this is so." Then she drooped again and I lifted her higher. She steadied herself on the table. "My apologies. Tis so dry . . ."

"I have water," I said. "Stay here."

The princess put both hands on the table and leaned against it. I stepped back, waited a second to see if she would topple, then hastily took off my pack and knelt on the floor.

"Food?" Urath asked hopefully, poking his rocky head into the doorway.

"I'm sorry, Urath. No more food." I grabbed my stainless steel water bottle and pulled it out. I offered it to the princess.

She accepted it and took two great gulps. With each one, she straightened a little more.

"Glorious." She stopped, looking longingly at the bottle, then at me. She offered it back. "Thou art too kind, but I shall not use the entirety of thy water . . ."

"Use it all," I said.

"In truth?"

"Uh, yes. In truth."

"And wouldst I offend thee if I did use it thus?" She held the bottle over her head.

"You want to pour it on your head?"

The princess smiled weakly. "In the land from whence I hail, we breathe water more than air."

I tried to remember what "hail" meant. That the princess came from there, I thought. Trying to follow her speech was like taking an English test. From the twelfth century.

The princess poured the water over her head. Her hair came alive, reaching up like tentacles, as if it was drinking. The sparkles in her hair gleamed, filling the room with soft blue light.

The princess sucked in a great breath like she had been suffocating. I looked for the puddle at her feet, but there wasn't one. The princess's body had soaked up the water like a sponge.

"Holey moley," I said.

The princess stood straight now, firmly on her feet. Her dark blue eyes sparkled.

"Many thanks, Lady . . ." she began, then trailed off, raising her blue eyebrows.

"Lorelei. I'm Lorelei."

"And I am Princess Ripellia. Thou might call me Ripple, an' it please thee." The princess dipped into an elegant curtsey.

I gave one back because, well, what do you do when someone curtseys to you? Except I was clumsy compared to her. Ripple's hands moved like reeds, and everything she did seemed part of a dance.

"Princess, we must get you out of here," Gruffy said. "Whatever fears you have, you may set them to rest. My companions and I shall protect you. Know that you walk with the greatest Doolivanti in all of Veloran."

"Indeed?" Ripple glanced at me, lashes low, but her gaze was intense. "Not a title lightly given," she said slowly. "Nor lightly accepted." She paused as though she expected something particular from me.

"I-I'm not . . . I don't even know what's going on here," I said. I wondered if Gruffy felt the need to compliment me just because I'd told him how brave he was.

Ripple turned back to Gruffy, and her intensity was gone. I wondered if anyone else had noticed it. She said, "Griffon and mouse, toucan and grimrock and Doolivanti, I am grateful for thy assistance. Thine interventions are most timely. I am able to travel, if thou art ready."

"Not a minute too soon. Not a minute too soon." Pip flapped overhead.

We started back up the dark hallway, and the softly glowing princess lit the tunnel. The walls shimmered blue, and I felt like I was underwater.

Excitement had begun to build inside me. If Gruffy was right about the princess being here, then he could be right about the Ink King and my family. And if we could rescue the princess, we could rescue them, too.

"Princess? I mean, um, your highness?"

"An' it please thee, thou might call me Ripple."

"I . . . Yes, okay. Ripple?"

"Yes, Milady Lorelei?"

"Your kingdom, it's called the Eternal Sea, right?"

"Indeed, milady."

"How did the Ink King take it?"

"With stealth and allies, milady. Ratsharks and Beetlins and great magic. A Doolivanti, he is."

"And are you a Doolivanti, too?"

"I am the Princess of the Eternal Sea. I am one with the waters of my birth."

"Um, okay. What does that mean?"

"Prithee, there are those who doth visit Veloran. Travelers, an' it please thee. Likewise, there are others, bright souls who are one with this land," she said. "Like thy griffon and toucan, thy mouse and grimrock."

"And you're one of those?"

"This body was birthed from the Eternal Sea, milady."

"Um, okay." I thought about that. I wasn't sure she'd really answered my question.

We wound around until we reached the place where I had first sent Gruffy home and pushed my way into Veloran. Aside from scuff marks on the sandy floor and the broken blocks in the wall Urath had hit with his fist, it could have been any other place in this winding, torch-lit hallway. I looked for any sign that there was a way back to my world. There was nothing, and I felt a sudden pang of fear. What if I couldn't get back? What if I was stuck here forever?

I pushed the thought away. It didn't matter. Find Theron, find my parents. That first, and the rest I could worry about after.

I turned my attention back to Ripple.

"When the Ink King did it, you know, when he took the Eternal Sea from you . . . did you see a little boy, nine years old? Did you see any grown-ups?" I asked.

"Grown-ups?"

"Adults. Parents. And the little boy is about this tall." I put my hand up to my chin. "With blond hair. He's really strong and, well . . . That's my family."

"Thourt intrepid to seek them so fervently, milady," the princess said. "I regret to say I have no news for thee. The Ink King struck fast. I saw nothing of his attack. Mine own memory extends only to a sharp blow in mine back. I didst see inky tentacles, then nothing 'tween that moment and this when thou didst wake me. Truly, I am sorry."

I nodded, feeling glum. "It's okay. I . . . It just would be nice to know I'm on the right track, you know?"

"Thy griffon friend hast utter faith in thee."

I glanced over at Gruffy. "Yeah," I said. "Yeah, he hast." Which was strange. Why was he such a big fan? That was another question that needed answering. We'd just met, but he kept talking about me like I was a celebrity or something.

Urath stopped, and we all pulled up short behind him. He put his hand out and the air suddenly crackled with black lightning. Fingers of black ooze slithered back and forth and solidified into a wall. The grimrock winced, yanked his hand back, and the wall faded.

"No can leave." Urath turned to me. "No can get more food."

I walked forward, but the wall was gone. Nothing stopped me from continuing up the tunnel. And Gruffy had flown right up this corridor after I gave my sandwich to Urath.

"There was no wall when I flew to get bread," Gruffy said, seeming to read my mind.

Worry furrowed the grimrock's brow. He looked down at

Ripple and lowered his huge hand in front of her, blocking her way. "No leave Urath. Leave Urath and take princess, Ink King punish."

I jogged back down the tunnel and put a hand on Urath's big arm. "I'm not leaving you, Urath."

"You fix," Urath said, and there was menace in his tone. "You set Urath free."

Gruffy watched me, then watched the grimrock. His talons gripped the sandy floor.

I walked up to the exact spot Urath had stood, closed my eyes, and put my hands in front of me, trying to find what had repelled the grimrock.

At first, I felt nothing. But then, slowly, my hands grew warmer. I followed the feeling.

The burn in my chest flared.

"Ow!" I winced.

"Doolivanti?"

"I'm fine," I said.

"Can go now?" Urath asked, reaching forward. The air crackled and spit sparks. Urath snatched his hand back. Inky fingers slithered in front of the grimrock, creating the black wall again.

"You promised!" he wailed, turning to me.

The wall slowly faded again.

"I am trying." I held up my hands. "Just wait."

With a low rumble in his chest, Urath sat back, but he did not look happy. He kept himself in front of the princess. Gruffy was rigid, alert. Ripple waited calmly, as though she had nothing to fear. Her gaze stayed on me.

I looked at all of their faces, then turned back to where the wall had appeared for Urath.

I had a hunch. I raised my hands as though I held a pencil, just like I had with Gruffy in my house, and I wrote on the air.

Lorelei could see the wall clearly.

The burn in my chest blossomed like a double-decker jalapeno sandwich.

My fingertips tingled, and I felt something hard. I opened my eyes and saw murky black bits of wall in little circles underneath my fingers.

"Stop it," hissed a dark voice.

I snapped my head up. Orange torchlight glinted off an oily black form slithering up the wall, then it was gone, lost in the shadows. "Loreliar . . ." Its voice stretched on each syllable. That was the same voice that had whispered to me in the dark!

"Beware, Doolivanti." Gruffy landed at my side, lowering his eagle head. "That is the Ink King."

"Oh yeah?" I turned toward him and balled up my fists.

The darkness chuckled. I couldn't see where the shadows stopped and the Ink King started. Was he a person or a spider or a snake? I couldn't see. I peered to try to get a better look.

"Oh, you're so tough," the voice hissed. "Make a fist and hide behind a griffon? Well, he's nothing." Black tentacles streaked out of the darkness. Gruffy screeched as he leapt forward, talons extended. But the tentacles wrapped around his front legs, binding them together. They continued, coiling around the griffon's wings, hindquarters, and finally his head. Gruffy fell to the floor like a sack of flour.

"Squeak!" exclaimed Squeak.

"Stop it!" I yelled.

"You're so stupid," the Ink King's voice echoed in the tunnel. "This is my world. What you make doesn't matter."

Inky tentacles unfurled from the blackness, grabbed me and lifted me off my feet. Behind me, the sandstone wall flickered gray. Lightning flashed beyond it, and I saw the window in my parents' bedroom.

"Doolivanti!" Gruffy shouted, struggling against the black bonds.

"Lady Lorelei!" Ripple cried.

The black tentacles threw me toward the light. I hurtled past Gruffy and Ripple like a softball.

"No!" I shouted. The last thing I saw was Pip's long beak as he flapped frantically toward me, then everything was gone.

I crashed onto the hardwood floor of my house. Dark, slanted walls hovered over me and the orange light of the hallway vanished. The thunderstorm rumbled outside the window. I was in my house again, right where I had been when I had followed Gruffy through to Veloran.

"No!" I sat up, craning my neck to look back at the wall, but someone was standing there. "Who—?"

A thin hand lanced down from above me and grabbed my arm.

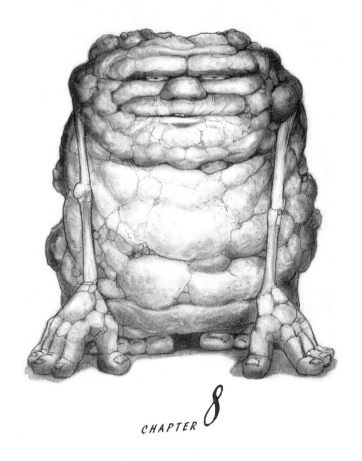

CHAPTER 8

A TEENAGE GIRL HAULED ME UPRIGHT. SHE WAS SLENDER, WITH bulgy green eyes and black bangs cut straight across her forehead. She looked like a frog with a pop-star haircut.

"Let go!" I yanked my arm, but her hands were like bones, and she was way stronger than she looked.

"Dad said you would try to come here," said Froggy Pop Star. "I wonder if he knew you'd be up here. Freak."

She dragged me toward the doorway on the opposite side of the room, the one that led to the staircase.

"This is my house!" I shouted, struggling. Froggy Pop Star bent my arm behind my back, and I gasped. Pain shot through my shoulder.

"Stop it, or I'll make it worse," she said through clenched teeth.

We went down the stairs awkwardly, reached the first floor, and she shoved me into the kitchen, making me trip and almost fall.

"Dad, it's the crazy girl. She was upstairs."

There was no one in the kitchen, and I got ready to bolt for the front, but a stooped figure blocked the doorway, hands together like a praying mantis. It was my psychiatrist!

"Mr. Schmindly!" I spat.

"Dr. Schmindly," he corrected me. He hated it when I called him "mister." But I would never call him doctor. Doctors were supposed to help people.

I felt like someone had put a pot next to my head and hit it with a hammer. My ears wouldn't stop ringing. Fear blossomed inside me. What if I was actually in a therapy session? What if I'd imagined Gruffy and all the rest?

I looked down at my arms. But no. The scratches were there from the fight with the grimrock. I had been in that corridor. Right?

I craned my neck to look back at the stairway to upstairs. I need to get to Veloran again. I tried to pull free, but Froggy Pop Star wrenched me around to face Mr. Schmindly.

We'd only had a few sessions together, and not a single one was helpful. From the beginning, he kept asking me about the night of the rainstorm, over and over about the tentacles, like he was looking for something, like he knew something more that he wasn't saying. He asked about the details, looking at me like I was three scoops of his favorite ice cream. But after our talks, he'd report out to Auntie Carrie and Uncle Jone about my "delusions" and "trauma." I begged Auntie Carrie not to send me to him anymore, and she finally agreed, even though Schmindly kept calling her to set up new appointments. I hadn't seen him for months.

He blinked behind his thick glasses. He had a gap in his gray front teeth, and he brought up a cigarette and sucked on it. In my house!

"What are you doing here?" I demanded.

He flicked an annoyed glance at his daughter. "Keep hold of her, Tabitha. She's quick." He turned his fake smile on me again. "We wouldn't want her running about, hurting herself."

Tabitha's hands tightened on my arms.

Mr. Schmindly seemed to relax. "How are you?" he asked in his nice voice. The fake voice. The voice he used to fool everyone. "It's been a long time since you've come to see me. Your aunt said you've been sick." He looked at me. "You don't look sick. You know, telling the truth to others helps you tell the truth to yourself. This is how we get better. You cannot change things by avoiding the truth."

"This is my house. Get out!" I said.

He chuckled, a horrible smoker's rasp. "You should thank me."

"For smoking in my house?"

He glanced at the cigarette, then shook his head. "I'm saving your house, Miss Lorelei. No one else wanted it. Old thing. See the cracks in the walls? They were going to tear it down and build a new one. But I saved it, took it as my own."

"You *bought* my house?" I felt light-headed.

Mr. Schmindly's bespeckled black eyes flicked back and forth, up and down, as though he was studying my left ear, then my right, then my hair, then my neck.

"You kept talking about how important your house is to you. So I figured there might be something here that I'd want to see." He smiled halfway, like he could barely make the effort to keep up the act. "And now here you are, sneaking around. Are you looking for something? A doorway, maybe?"

I felt cold. Doorway. He knew about Veloran. Crumpling creepers. Veloran *was* real, and Mr. Schmindly knew all about it. That's why he kept calling to get appointments with me. Not to help me, but because he wanted what I knew. What he *thought* I knew. All this time, he thought I knew where my family had gone, and he was trying to find out more. Except I hadn't known, so he'd never been able to get it out of me.

Frustrating for him, I bet. The big, skinny smokestack.

He leaned forward, hands clasped together in front of his chest. Smoke curled up from the cigarette stuck between his fingers. A flake of ash fell on my floor.

"You've been there, haven't you?" Mr. Schmindly said, his eyes lighting up as he looked at me. "I can see it."

I swallowed. "Um, been upstairs?"

"Clever," he said, ignoring my totally lame lie. "To the Wishing World. Did you see my son?" Yeah, right. If Mr. Schmindly had a Doolivanti son, he was probably the Ink King.

"I knew it," Tabitha said. "The little bug-head made it."

"Of course he did," Mr. Schmindly said. "I told him how."

"You told me how, too. Like that helped," Tabitha retorted.

"You have to have imagination to be invited to Veloran, Tabitha," Mr. Schmindly said, flicking a derisive glance over my head at her. "Obviously that was too much to ask of you." I snuck a look up at her. Her lips were pressed together so firmly that they were a straight line. Now she looked even more like a frog.

"This sounds like a family argument," I said. "I'll come back some other time." I tested, pulling against Tabitha's grip again. She yanked me back in front of her.

"What are you looking for here?" Mr. Schmindly asked. "Something from the Wishing World, maybe? Something you left behind?"

If I was as strong as Theron, I could have done something. Even at nine years old, he could out-wrestle fourth and fifth graders. He could tackle a grown man. He could have twisted out of skinny Tabitha's grip, knocked Mr. Schmindly down, and run right over him.

I'd have to go a different way, make up a better story. I hung my head, tried to look dejected.

"Yeah. I had to get something my Dad left me," I said.

Mr. Schmindly's eyes got wider, and a smile crooked his thin lips. "Tell me about this thing."

I didn't know why he wanted to get to Veloran, but he was so eager that he was shaking. And that pretty much meant there was no way he should *ever* go there.

"It's a rock," I said. "A piece of rock my Dad gave me, said it was from the comet. About this big." I held up my hands as though I was holding a basketball.

"Narolev's Comet." Mr. Schmindly nodded. "Yes. Go on."

"Well, I hid it in the house. That's why I came back."

"Excellent. This is real progress, Lorelei." He put the nasty cigarette to his lips and sucked, blew out smoke. "Now, tell me where you hid it." The smoke wafted out of his mouth around the words.

"In the vent cover."

His smile widened, and his hands trembled. If he knew I was wearing one of Dad's "comet stones" under my shirt right now, he would've snatched it right off me. I felt the need to grab it, but I kept my hands tight by my sides.

The stones were linked to the comet. The comet was linked to Veloran.

"Which," he said, and took a little gulp of air as though he couldn't quite catch his breath. "Vent cover?"

"In-in the dining room."

"Excellent, Lorelei. Excellent. You're a charming child." He turned and disappeared from view.

I had to get out of here. I had to tell Auntie Carrie and Uncle Jone.

I heard him thump to his knees to take off the vent cover. It didn't lead to a vent, like a normal vent cover would. My house was a hundred years old, and things didn't always do what they had been made to do. Mom and Dad called it "quirky."

So the vent—which should have connected to the heater—went straight down to the dirt foundation. There was a crawl space underneath the house, dark and dirty and full of old things from a hundred years ago: steel bands and broken glass, ancient two-by-fours and tiny barrels of century-old glue. Not to mention a lot of spiders. Mr. Schmindly would have to put his arm all the way into the hole. He'd have to stretch to even touch the dirt, get down on his belly.

It would be hard for him to get up quickly from that position.

I raised my heel and stomped as hard as I could on the top of Tabitha's foot.

She screamed, and her grip went soft. I swung my elbows left and right and connected with something hard. Her head, maybe. She gave a muffled cry and fell back.

I shot forward, skirting the kitchen island and dashing for the dining room. I knew how to work the locks at top speed from running away from Theron during our games. I'd be out on the street in a second—

Mr. Schmindly's foot smacked into my shins.

I tripped and sprawled onto the living room floor. My elbows and knees hit the hardwood and I cried out.

I scrambled to my feet, gritting my teeth, and lunged again for the door, but Mr. Schmindly caught my ankle and yanked me backward. My chin hit the floor, and I saw stars.

His hand closed on my arm, squeezing hard.

"Clever," he said, breathing hard. He staggered to his feet and hauled me up with him. "But you're not helping yourself. Lies are bad for you." A hacking cough wracked him, and he put a fist to his mouth until it stopped. "We could work together, Lorelei. Just you think about that. Show me what I want, and we could be friends."

"We'll never be friends!" I shouted.

Tabitha limped into view with a hand to her mouth. Blood

leaked between her fingers. "Vuu liffle momfter! Im kim you!" She started forward, but Mr. Schmindly shook his head, using his counselor's voice again.

"She's eleven, Tabitha. Really? You couldn't hold onto her?"

"Shuff fup!"

"Put some ice on it." Mr. Schmindly looked down at me. "Now, little Miss Lorelei. We need to work on your honesty. Is the comet stone really in the vent?"

I struggled, but I couldn't get free. "It's buried down there."

"How deep?"

"All the way to China! Let me go!" I tried to punch him.

He grunted, caught my fist, and held it. "You're like my boy," he said through his teeth. "Entitlement. You think the Wishing World belongs to you. Well, it doesn't. I worked my whole life to find a way back. I counseled children so I could hear their dreams, hoping for the keys to unlock the door again. I taught my ungrateful son everything I knew, everything I remembered. Now you and he have both found a way, and I'm not going to stand by while you leave me behind."

Slowly and deliberately, he intertwined his fist into my hair and pulled my head back so hard tears came to my eyes.

"Ow!"

"Don't struggle, and it won't hurt," he lied, walking me to the kitchen.

We passed Tabitha, who glared at me over a paper towel filled with ice.

He opened the old basement door and shoved me through. The stairs were narrow and steep. It was all I could do to catch my balance and not crash headfirst into the concrete wall at the bottom.

Mr. Schmindly slammed the door and it went dark.

"You sit down there and think about your lies. When you are ready to dig up the comet stone and bring it to me, I will let you out. I'm tired of being nice. To you, to my son. To all selfish children. No more. We must create a space of trust between us. We must tell each other the truth. Do you understand?"

I blinked against the darkness and let my eyes adjust. Light trickled in through cracks where the door met the floor. I moved farther down into the basement, which had always given me the creeps. This buried room felt like it was about to fall in on itself. Bulging brick walls held back the dirt and created a sunken space that adults could barely stand up in. Heater vent pipes, water pipes, and electrical wires ran overhead alongside the tall, thick boards that held up the floor.

I pulled my necklace out and held it up.

A flicker of orange light sparked in the corner by the hot water heater, a flash of yellow stones and a sandy floor. I drew a breath.

I let go of the necklace. The orange light faded.

"It's true . . ." I whispered. The necklace did have something to do with Veloran.

I closed my eyes, holding up my hand like it had a pencil. I held onto the necklace with my other hand. I thought of the golden sandstone of the tunnel. The soft feathers at Gruffy's neck.

This is my story, I thought, and I felt a thrill in my belly. I could do magic. I didn't know why, or how. Whatever the reason, a hundred Mr. Schmindlys weren't going to keep me in this basement.

I held up my hand, writing the words out in front of myself with an imaginary pencil.

Lorelei returned to Veloran and defeated the Ink King.

The words burned on the air, then fell away one letter at a time, rushing at the faint portal, making it brighter, clearer, deeper. Flickering torchlight and stone blocks painted themselves across the air.

I stepped into it, felt that invisible film against me, heard the whisper that wanted to change me into the Loremaster, but it was weaker this time. I shrugged through it, ignored the voice, and it felt like someone was striking a match inside my rib cage.

CHAPTER *9*

I APPEARED BACK WHERE I'D FIRST ENTERED VELORAN. THE grimrock's fist scar marred the wall to my right. The sandy floor, scuffed from the battle, was underneath my feet. I looked up the hallway. I couldn't see anyone, but I heard them.

"Urath." The Ink King's voice echoed from up ahead. "You swore to keep everyone away from the princess. You failed. Now you can starve!"

"Nooooo!" Urath moaned.

I kicked it into gear and ran up the hall.

"What do we do? What do we do?" came Pip's identifiable squawk.

"We defeat this villain," Gruffy said, his voice muffled. He must still be tied up in the Ink King's tentacles. It was like I had just left, even though I'd been with Mr. Schmindly and Froggy Pop Star for at least twenty minutes.

I had to think of something. I wasn't about to let the Ink King kill my new friends. A girl only gets so many friends. And honestly, how often are they griffons and talking toucans and mice?

But he was so powerful! I'd barely had time to say, "Stick it in your ear!" before he tossed me through the magic doorway.

Still, I had been onto something before I got tossed out of Veloran. I had found the Ink King's wall, and I could have undone it if he hadn't showed up. I had been this close! The story I had written had started to happen. Rather than months of telling myself I could do pull-ups and straining through them, I had made the wall appear just like that.

A wish maker, Gruffy had said. *A Doolivanti.*

I slowed my jog and crept around the bend.

Urath moaned in fear, pushing his giant hands against his little head. Ripple stood calmly beside him, and her all-blue gaze turned to look at me as though she'd been expecting me.

Okay. So that's weird.

The Ink King had come out of the shadows, and I saw now that he was a person. Kind of. He was oily black, like someone my size had been dipped in tar, except with a hundred tentacles stretching out from him. He clung to the wall, hanging in the midst of his tentacles like a boy-spider, just beyond where Gruffy lay bound and struggling. The Ink King's cocky voice said it all: he had this fight all wrapped up.

Wrap this up, I thought.

I drew a breath and wrote on the air.

The Ink King fell on his big inky butt and ran away from Lorelei and her friends.

"Girl said she free Urath!" The grimrock turned away from the Ink King, his chest heaving. His hands balled into fists. "Girl left Urath alone!"

"I didn't leave." I walked into the open as the words I had written burned and peeled away, flying toward the Ink King. They disappeared, but nothing seemed to happen.

"Lady Lorelei!" Ripple exclaimed. Okay, a little more weird, please? Hadn't she already seen me? Why the shock and awe?

"I sent you away!" the Ink King exclaimed.

"And I came back," I said.

"This is my world!" he said. Several black tentacles pointed at me.

Okay magic, I thought. *Now would be a good time to kick in—*

"Whulp!" Tentacles reached out from the shadows behind me and grabbed my ankles. My feet skidded on the ground as I fought them.

The Ink King gestured and images appeared in the ink that swirled in front of me.

We can't find them, the police said, three of them standing over me, as tall as the grimrock.

They're gone, Auntie Carrie whispered from my side, also larger than she should be. *I don't know why. But they're gone. We have to move on . . .*

Three of my friends from school stood on the shoulders of the police. *Does that make you an orphan now?* They all asked together.

They must have abandoned her . . . the police said.

They're not coming back. We're going to have to sell the house. Auntie Carrie hung her head.

The images rose over me and toppled, and I stumbled backward. Behind me, I could see the furnace in my basement as though it was painted on the sandstone wall. My feet slid on the sand as I was pulled toward it.

Suddenly, the Ink King gasped; Squeak had bit down on his oily black foot. The charcoal mouse scurried back and a bright spot of blood welled up on the Ink King's toe.

"Stupid rat!" The Ink King flailed, stumbling back and falling onto his butt. His tentacles flung out, pushed him back upright, and he kicked out at Squeak.

Squeak dodged the kick, stood up on his hind legs, and did a little victory dance.

The tentacles that bound me went slack. I yanked my right hand free enough to scribble on my leg.

Head on head.

The words burned and peeled. Fire flared in my chest. I gasped, then slammed my head forward.

The Ink King staggered, reeling as though I had head-butted him.

That's it, magic, I thought. *That's what I'm talking about.*

The tunnel rumbled. Dust sifted down from above.

I stood up straight and sucked in a breath. The tentacles slithered away into the shadows and all of the Ink King's images blurred. The policemen, my friends at school, Auntie Carrie, and Theron all slipped into the darkness like water down a drain.

"I'm staying here," I yelled.

The Ink King backed away.

I walked up to the place where Urath's invisible wall should be and reached out my hand. I felt it right away, but instead of little circles around my fingers, the blackness extended out from my whole hand.

I carved my sentence on the wall like I had a knife.

This wall is broken.

It shattered. Black glass blew apart, falling like rain and skittering across the floor. A fiery fingernail raked inside me from belly to breastbone.

I stood in the rubble, trying not to wince as I stared down the Ink King. "Where are my parents?" I said.

The dark-on-dark eyes watched me.

With a screech, Gruffy burst out of his shadow bonds. He unfurled his wings and launched himself at the Ink King, but the villain slithered backward so fast I could barely see him.

"You think you're so strong, griffon," the Ink King hissed. "Follow me and find out."

"Squeak!"

Gruffy landed on the ground, searching overhead.

"Squeak is right. Squeak is right," Pip squawked. "Stay out of the shadows. Out of the shadows."

"Come after me, stupid griffon. See what happens to you."

"Better to brace him now than later." Gruffy strode into the dark.

"No!" I had a terrible feeling about Gruffy going after the Ink King in the dark.

"Chase me, griffon . . ." The Ink King's slithery whisper echoed in the tunnel, but I couldn't see him.

"Let him go, Gruffy," I begged. "Please."

Gruffy turned, paused for a long moment, then he bowed to me. "As you wish, Doolivanti."

CHAPTER *10*

WE CONTINUED UP THE TUNNEL, AND I PEERED INTO EACH shadow. The Ink King did not come back. But I did notice little bumps on the walls about the size of my fist. One of them popped out and became a sandy hand.

"Eeep!" I squeaked and jumped back. It reached for me as though to shake hands.

"What is that?" I said.

"Shake and bake. Shake and bake," Pip said.

"Go ahead. They will not hurt you," Gruffy assured me.

I reached out and took the sand hand. It shook mine vigorously and then sucked back into the wall and became a bump again just as another extended. I shook it. Another and another and another popped out, all eager for their turn. Ripple moved forward and began shaking them, too.

"Okay, I get the shake part. What's the bake part?" I asked.

"The hot air of Azure City," Gruffy said, flapping upward. He opened a big wooden trapdoor in the ceiling. Blinding yellow sunlight lit the tunnel and a blast of heat followed.

"Hoppin' hot potatoes," I murmured. I let go of the hand I was shaking, and they all stuck out of the wall, beckoning me. I stepped forward, putting my foot on one of their hands as I grabbed another. They lifted me up through the trapdoor and set me on the sand above. They did the same for Ripple and Squeak, who hopped deftly up their flat hands like steps. Gruffy and Pip flew out. Urath simply reached up to the edges of the trapdoor and pulled himself out, *thooming* onto the packed yellow earth one bony knee at a time. He shielded his eyes.

"Thanks Shake and Bake!" I said to the hands. They all waved good-bye.

I squinted, and a huge, golden city came into focus. There were buildings and towers, all made of sand. Some were small, square houses. Some were castle turrets without the rest of the castle. Some looked like skyscrapers. There were slides everywhere, carrying water from one place to another, and between all of the tallest buildings were sandstone walkways like golden ropes.

I turned, trying to take it all in. I mean, my first seconds in Veloran were chock full of fantastical creatures, but this was amazing in a totally different way. The city went on and on. One giant sprawl of sand castles of all shapes and sizes.

"Who built this?" I asked in a hushed tone.

"Sand Spinner. Sand Spinner," Pip said.

"And that would be a Doolivanti?" I guessed, thinking of the names he'd run past me when I first introduced myself.

"What else? What else?" Pip said.

Okay, I thought. Mental note: creatures can be all sizes and types and possess in-born abilities. Like a toucan talking. Or a man made all of rock. But Doolivantis are builders, magicians. They could make tentacles out of shadows. Skyscrapers out of sand.

Sculpted fountains floated through the streets, pouring sand onto the ground. People walked around them, but every now and then, someone would approach the foundation and put a bucket underneath, and then the sand turned to water until the bucket was filled.

"Whompin' waterbuckets," I murmured. I thought of what Mr. Schmindly had said to his daughter, about needing to have imagination to come to Veloran. Well, the Sand Spinner had it in spades.

Urath held his arms up, trying to hide himself from the sun. "Too bright."

"The grimrock cannot remain long," Gruffy said. "We must find him a cool place, with shade."

"And the princess. And the princess," said Pip.

"An' I but have a modicum of water, I shall be fine," Ripple said, but she looked like she was wilting.

"What about those?" I pointed at the closest floating sand fountain. "Think it will turn into water if you stand under it?"

"I know not."

"Let's know so." I marched over to the fountain. Whatever magic held it aloft sensed me coming and turned toward me. It moved gently, as though its only purpose was to be useful.

Ripple neared; she squinted up at the pouring sand that left piles on the street. "Thou art certain?"

I laughed. "No. But it turns to water for everyone else. Why not us?"

Ripple closed her eyes and stepped under the stream of sand. It immediately turned to water, splashing over her head. She gasped and turned her face up into it, letting it cascade over her. Like when she had poured my water bottle over her head, not a single drop touched the ground. I waited for the princess to swell up like a balloon, but instead, she flung her arms out and spun. Her sparkling gown whirled out, growing three times as wide as Ripple was tall, as though it had soaked up all the water that wasn't falling onto the sand.

With a deep breath, she pirouetted out from under the stream, her face turned toward the sun. She looked gloriously bright and alive.

"Wow!" I said.

"Ah, Mother Water. Thou art most refreshing!" She sighed, then looked at me. "I knew not how weak I was 'til I was infused with her life once more."

"If you've had a good drink, we'd best get moving. Best get moving," Pip said, looking at the villagers staring at Urath.

"Squeak," Squeak agreed.

I squinted up the hill, fascinated by all the amazing buildings. I could explore this place for a week! The water slides all came from an enormous palace that had giant eyes all over its walls. They blinked down at the rest of the city. "Look at that!" I said.

"Eyes of the Sand Spinner. Eyes of the Sand Spinner," Pip replied.

"And all the water comes from there. Is there a huge fountain or something? Or a river?"

"The Sand Spinner supplies water for all of Azure City," Gruffy said.

"But where does it come from?" I asked.

"Am I to know?" Gruffy replied.

"Does it matter? Does it matter?" Pip asked.

They began moving down the street away from the palace. I looked at all the eyes for one long moment. "Aren't you curious at all?"

"It is what it is," Gruffy said.

That seemed like a very poor answer, but top priority was to get Urath some shade, so I gave Azure City one long look, then turned and followed them. I'd come back here.

We got scared looks from everyone we passed. People scurried out of our way, slammed their doors. The enormous golden gates at the city's outer wall were open. The guards on top of the wall scrambled to the edge and gaped down from their perch. They didn't know what to do about Urath. If a grimrock had been trying to enter the city from outside, I was sure they'd have closed the gates, but since he was already inside—and apparently leaving—they just stood there and let him walk out.

Outside the city lay a desert. Sort of. The sand only stretched for about a hundred feet before changing to a lush, grassy pasture speckled with trees.

"Are you kidding me?" I asked, jogging the length of the sandy stretch. There was actually a line between the desert and the pasture. I stopped, one foot on sand, one on grass. On one side, it was hot and bright. On the other, cool and moist. I could feel each half on each side of my face.

"The desert just ends," I said.

"Yes," Gruffy replied.

"How can it do that?"

"It has always been this way."

"Always? You live here?"

"No, Doolivanti. We arrived earlier today for the first time, looking for the princess."

I screwed up my lips to keep from laughing. "So it has *always* been this way as of a few hours ago?"

Gruffy looked at me like he didn't understand the question.

"Always," I tried to clarify. "You said always. But you've only been here a few hours. How is that always?"

"I feel you are somehow disappointed, Doolivanti," Gruffy said.

"I just want to know why there's a line in the sand here. Literally!"

"Because it has always been this way."

"Always? How do you know?"

"It was that way ever since we have been here," he said.

I opened my mouth to retort, but I stopped. I couldn't really make him know something he didn't. And I obviously couldn't make him curious about it.

"Never mind," I said.

"Follow me. Follow me." Pip flapped overhead. "Squeak knows a ravine that will work for Urath. Will work for Urath."

We started walking, and I moved over to Ripple, who seemed to enjoy the pasture and forest much more than the desert. I had some questions for her, too.

She looked up at me with that calm expression. "Milady Lorelei."

"I caught you looking at me," I said.

"Milady?" she asked.

"When I came back. You saw me, but you didn't say anything. Then when I walked out into the open, you exclaimed my name as though you were surprised."

She paused, then said. "Indeed, milady. Twas that not what you wished?"

"What *I* wished?"

"Didst thou not wish to give surprise to the Ink King? Prithee, I didst as I thought thou wouldst wish. Thy return was my most fervent desire, and I didst quell mine own excitement 'til all had viewed thee, lest I give away thy presence to our foe."

I frowned. I was a little disappointed that that actually made sense. But . . .

"So you were trying to keep me hidden until I chose to show myself?"

"Of course, milady."

"Um, okay." I could have sworn she had looked at me as if to say: *there she is, right on time.* But maybe I was wrong. It had all been very fast. I changed the subject.

"So does the Ink King live in Azure City?" I asked.

"I think not," Ripple said.

"Likely the fiend resides in the Eternal Sea," Gruffy interjected, swooping down and landing next to us. Squeak rode on top of the griffon's head. Pip had ranged far in front of the group, perhaps looking for the ravine.

"Our fine griffon dost speak truth. He shall not easily give up the Eternal Sea."

"And that's where we're going," I said. "If my family is in Veloran, they'll be where the Ink King is. Right?"

"Of course," Gruffy said. "We take Urath to a safe place, then to the Eternal Sea."

"All right then," I said.

We walked until the sun began setting, and I marveled at the landscape. Lush grass and bright sun. It was warm like the best days of summer. The pretty little trees looked like they had been made just to make you feel happy, and the path curved toward the horizon like a smile.

"What is this place?" I asked.

"Greenleave," Gruffy said.

"It's so different than Azure City."

"Twas made by the Leaf Laugher."

Another Doolivanti, I thought. "And he made all this?"

"She did. Yes, of course."

"She. Sorry. Okay," I said. "And I can do this, too?" I rubbed my chest in memory of the burning. I wondered if other Doolivantis had similar pain when they used their powers.

"Not this," Gruffy said.

"What? Why not this?"

Gruffy looked at me as though he didn't understand. "Well, because you are not the Leaf Laugher, of course."

More mental notes: Doolivantis expressed in different ways. "So the Sand Spinner couldn't make Greenleave?" I asked.

"He would not want to. He is the master of sand."

"Right. But if he wanted to, he could."

"He would not."

"But he could."

"How could one do that which one would not do?" Gruffy said, looking at me with a frown.

"I . . ." When he said it like that, it did sound confusing. "Never mind," I said.

"Here we are. Here we are," Pip squawked.

Before us stretched a deep, gray ravine. The granite shone with moisture and the bottom was so deep it disappeared into darkness.

Urath slammed his fists happily on the ground and, without a word to any of us, ran down into the growing shadows without a backward glance.

"Hey!" I called after him, then turned to Gruffy. "He didn't even say good-bye."

"You got a grimrock to not squash us. Not squash us. Be glad. Be glad," Pip answered.

"Well, I sure hope there's a lot of food down there," I said. "He's going to go through it in a hurry."

Pip chuckled, which sounded like pieces of chalk clinking together.

My stomach grumbled, and I thought it sure would be great to have one of my grimrock-devoured peanut butter and jelly sandwiches right about now.

We found a place to sleep a short distance away by a gurgling brook. Gruffy was pretty good at picking a campsite, I had to admit. And he collected firewood faster than anyone I'd ever met. He was really good at spotting it. His eyes were amazing. Pip found a whole tree of walnuts, and that's what we had for dinner.

The grass was so soft that I was looking forward to spending the night out under the stars. Pip found a lone tree and landed on one of its branches. He inspected it thoroughly, as though there might be too many knots or something, then settled down. Ripple went to the brook. She gurgled back to it as she put her toes in, breathed a long sigh, then laid down underneath the water. Her living hair sparkled with little stars.

I watched that for a minute. She didn't come up for a breath. So cool.

I walked away from the fire into the dark and looked up at the strange night sky. Long white streaks stretched in parallel lines from one side of the sky to the other. They weren't soft and cloudy like the Milky Way; they were more like the trails of a jet plane. Except enormous. And glowing. At night. There was nothing else up there. No moon, no stars, nothing except those streaks.

No, wait. I squinted at a section close to the treetops and I thought I could see something round behind the streaks. It was a moon, maybe, but it was hard to be sure. I got tired of squinting and looked away. My eyes were then drawn to the only other thing in the sky: a burning red line that hung just above the horizon. It was ragged and angry, like someone had ripped open the sky. I shivered.

"Psst."

I spun around. Behind me, shielded from the firelight by a

tall boulder, stood a boy my own age. His red hair was shaved close on the sides, with a tangled twist on top. Prominent freckles spotted his face.

"You scared me!" I said. He looked familiar. I'd seen him somewhere before.

"Come here," he whispered.

I looked back toward Gruffy, far away. He wasn't looking this way—

"Don't do that," the boy commanded, shaking his head. He motioned me behind the boulder, away from the light.

"Do I know you?" I asked.

"'Course you do. Come here."

"Why?"

He let out an exasperated sigh. "'Cause you don't know what you're doing, and I can help you."

"Who are you?"

"Do you know where you are?" He answered my question with a question.

"Um," I said. "Veloran."

He shook his head. "That's what the animals call it. This is the Wishing World."

"The Wishing World?" That's what Mr. Schmindly had called it, back at my house. I wondered if all Doolivantis called it the Wishing World.

"Yes."

"Okay." I put my hands on my hips. "So?" Where had I seen this kid? He wasn't in my class at my old school or in my new one near Auntie Carrie and Uncle Jone's house.

"So you gotta do certain things first." He paused, motioned me into the shadows again. "Come here and I'll tell you how it works."

I hesitated a moment, then joined him behind the boulder, just at the edge of the light.

"You think you're in a dream?" he asked, his voice quieter.

"Pretty sure I'm not," I said.

"Well, you aren't. This is a different place, as real as Earth. More real, even."

"Okay."

"You can die here, you know," he said darkly.

I glanced over my shoulder. My friends were far away, and none of them were watching me. Gruffy poked at the fire with a stick clutched in his talon. Pip's head was tucked under his wing. Squeak had laid down on a rock near the fire and looked asleep. Ripple was still beneath the water. I couldn't even see her from here.

"Tell me who you are," I said.

"I'm Jimmy."

It came to me then. He *had* been at my school, my old school. I'd seen him at that horrible spelling bee where I'd botched the word "leviathan" in front of everyone. When I had walked back from the line of contestants at the front of the gymnasium, this boy had been last in the line. He had grinned as though my humiliation was his success.

"You were at that spelling bee where I lost."

He paused. "Right," he said in a monotone. "The spelling bee where *you* lost."

I didn't much like him then. And I didn't much like him now. "Gruffy says this is Veloran," I said.

"The griffon," he said, his voice flat, "doesn't know anything."

I frowned, and he continued. "Seriously. He's a paper cutout. A video game character. The griffon doesn't have a soul. He doesn't care who you are, where you are. Ask him, you'll see. Or the bird or the mouse." He paused, pressed his lips together. "Or the princess. They don't matter."

I didn't say anything.

He sighed. "Don't you get it? The Wishing World gives you whatever you want."

"Like a dream."

"Better than a dream. What dream gives you everything you want?"

"Okay." I closed my eyes and concentrated. "I just wished for what I wanted. And nothing happened."

His face went stony. "Don't make fun of me."

"I just think you're lying."

"I'm not. You can have what you want, but you have to see it first."

"See it?" I asked.

"Do you want your parents or don't you?"

Cold shivered up my back and I stepped away from him. "How do you know I'm looking for my parents?"

"Because . . ." He paused, let out a frustrated growl. "Because of course you are. Aren't you? You're the girl who lost her parents. On the news, right?"

I paused. "Okay, yes."

"Okay, then. You want to find them?"

"I think the Ink King has them," I said.

He paused. "Then you *so* need my help. The Ink King is the most powerful Doolivanti in the Wishing World."

I wasn't sure I wanted anything from this boy, but he did seem to know a lot.

"Okay then," I said.

"So you want your parents. That's your wish, right? So go to the Starfield. Everyone sees their wish there. You look down into it, and it shows you what you want and how to get it. That's the way the Wishing World knows what to do for you, and it'll help you get to the Ink King if that's who has your parents. And it'll show you how to beat him."

"Starfield? Where is it?"

"Over there." He pointed.

I looked, but couldn't see anything except the white streaks overhead and the red rip in the sky. I looked back at Jimmy. "You're telling me that the one place I need is right next to where we camped?"

"That's the way the Wishing World works." He smiled smugly.

"So, you went to the Starfield?"

He was silent a moment, then said, "Of course."

"What did you want?"

He backed into the shadows behind the boulder. All I could see was his freckled nose. "Look, I'm just trying to help you, but you don't seem to care. I'm not going to waste any more time on you. If you want the Wishing World to work for you, you'll go to the Starfield."

Then he was gone.

I thought about chasing him, but didn't. Instead, I went back to the fire. Gruffy was preening, running long feathers through his beak.

Jimmy was from Earth, like me. How many Earth children were in Veloran?

"Gruffy," I said.

He stopped and looked up at me.

"How many others like me are in Veloran?" I asked. "Other Doolivantis? Are there a lot?"

"Doolivantis are rare."

"How many?"

"Am I to know?"

I let out a little breath and looked up at the sky, then I tried a different question. "What are the white stripes in front of the moon?"

"The sky," Gruffy said simply. "They are always there, though the moons are ever changing."

"Moons?"

"Indeed. Sometimes there is only one moon. Sometimes there are many."

"How many?"

"Sometimes four. Sometimes they are red. Or white. Sometimes green or yellow. The blue moon has been here for several days."

I could barely see the moon behind the white streaks, but it could be blue. Gruffy certainly had better eyes than I did. "How is that possible?"

He looked at me again like he had when I'd asked about the Azure City's aqueducts and where the water came from. "Am I to know?"

"What about that red rip in the sky?" I asked.

He looked up at the red line. "That is new."

"New? Aren't you curious where it came from?"

"Am I to know?" He continued his feather work. I remembered Jimmy's comment on my friends. Gruffy didn't care, didn't want to think about the reasons behind things.

"I suppose not," I said.

I got up and walked to the edge of the clearing, back toward the boulder where I had met Jimmy, then farther in the direction he had pointed.

The grass gave way to a lake of black glass. Underneath the surface, stars winked. I touched it with the toe of my purple running shoe. It was hard as rock. The Starfield.

I stepped onto it and didn't fall in. Wow!

I started walking, looking down. Some of the stars were large and others tiny, as though far away, deep beneath the surface. I kept going until I was in the middle and looked at the stars all around me. Under my feet!

I looked up at the white-striped sky, and then back down. Was this where the Wishing World kept its stars?

"Gruffy!" I called. "Look at this!"

Gruffy's head came up. He was really far away now. I had been so fascinated by the Starfield I hadn't even realized how far.

"Doolivanti?" he called.

"Did you see this? It's like black glass with all the universe inside. It's—"

I took a step toward him, but the ground beneath me leapt upward. A pillar of the starry black glass separated from the lake and shot straight up, taking me with it. The force pushed me flat on my belly. I struggled to my hands and knees. Above me, the flowing white lines of the sky came closer. I was moving as fast as a speeding car!

"Doolivanti!" Gruffy yelled from far below. He flapped fiercely toward me, but he shrank as the pillar rushed upward faster.

I sucked in a breath. The white streaks were almost upon me. The pillar was going to shove me into space!

"No!" I yelled. "Stop!"

The rising column of black stuttered, as though it had heard me, but continued upward.

I scratched a single word on the starry glass of the platform. *Stop.*

The burn in my chest flared, so hot I gasped.

"I said stop!" I breathed. The column gave a whimper, then stopped just at the edge of the shimmering white streaks.

Wincing, I massaged my breastbone, stood and looked up. The white streaks were so close. I reached up and brushed a finger across them. Sparkles fizzed around my hand, tickling. I stepped to the edge of the column and looked down. The ground was so far away it made me dizzy.

"Doolivanti!" Gruffy called from a great distance below. He was just a speck. I was higher in the air than I'd ever been, even in an airplane.

"I'm okay!" I yelled, stepping back from the edge. "I'm okay!" I think.

The pillar shuddered again, as though it wanted to keep going up. "No!" I said. It gave another whimper, but didn't do anything.

I looked up into the blackness of space, past the white streaks, which were like lines of snow blown over a mountain ridge. I could see the stars now, and they were shockingly close. I didn't know how I could even breathe. Somehow, though, I knew that if I slipped past the barrier of the white streaks, that would be it for me.

I looked over at the blue moon. White clouds swirled across its surface, and I could see—

I clapped a hand to my mouth.

"That's no moon," I murmured. I could see continents: Africa, Europe, Antarctica . . .

I looked to my left, following the white streaks. They flowed into one long line, stretching far out into the darkness.

"Whizzing wombats," I murmured. "I'm on the comet . . ."

I swallowed hard and stared at the blackness of space, at my entire planet like a big marble in the distance. Jimmy's words echoed in my head.

It's as real as Earth. More real, even. You can die here.

I knelt down, put my hand on the hard glass of the pillar, feeling the need to be on solid ground.

"Take me down," I whispered. Nothing happened.

Down. I traced the word on the glass, clenching my teeth at the burn that filled me.

The Starfield obeyed with a final whimper.

When the pillar came level with Gruffy, he flew protectively beside me, but the Starfield delivered me safely to the ground.

"Are you all right, Doolivanti?" Gruffy landed next to me and we walked back to our camp.

I was in a daze, and I didn't know what to say. The Ink King had said I didn't belong here. Was that why the Starfield tried to shoot me at the Earth instead of showing me how to reach my dreams?

We arrived at the fire and, without another word, Gruffy turned around once, then crouched down as though nothing had happened. I laid back on the grass, looking up at the streaked sky and holding onto the necklace Dad had given me.

Narolev's Comet. Narolev. I turned over and wrote the word out in the grass, saw it in my mind. I turned it around.

Narolev. Veloran.

Narolev was Veloran spelled backward!

I rolled over and stared up at the white streaks, at the barely visible Earth beyond them. Colossal cometoids! I was actually flying through space.

It made this place real in a way it hadn't felt before. I mean, the idea that I was in a magical dimension was one thing. It was like imagining I was in a picture with fuzzy edges. But thinking that I was hurtling through the unforgiving airlessness of space, that put a hard edge to everything. Even scientists acknowledged that Narolev's Comet was real, and that's where I was. The thought swam around and around in my head. Around and around . . .

Sleep eventually got me, but I dreamed of rocketing through the stars.

CHAPTER *11*

I WOKE TO ANGRY VOICES. WHAT THE WHAT? I BLINKED AND looked at the sky. The white streaks had faded and the sun was bright. It was morning.

"We already freed her. Already freed her," Pip was squawking. "That was the mission. That was the mission. And you almost got killed. Almost got killed!"

"Squeak."

I shook the sleep away and stood up.

"The Ink King has stolen the Doolivanti's family. The Eternal

Sea darkens daily," Gruffy said. "Such injustice cannot be borne. We shall go there. We shall brace him."

"This isn't a game. Isn't a game," Pip squawked.

Gruffy lifted his head, his feathers rising around his neck. "I am playing no game. We do what must be done. There is no other—"

"You're already in trouble. Already in trouble."

"What price I must pay is beside the point."

"Wait. What sort of trouble?" I asked, walking up to them as I rubbed sleep out of my eyes.

Gruffy shook his head. "It is nothing—"

"They'll ground you for life. Ground you for life."

Squeak chittered, smoothing out his whiskers.

"Enough, Pip!" Gruffy said.

"Your parents?" I asked.

"Your father will pull out your flight feathers. He'll pull out your flight feathers."

Then it dawned on me, but that was ridiculous! "Wait. You're not an adult griffon? But you're enormous!"

"Compared to his father, Gruffy's a sparrow. He's a sparrow."

Squeak chittered again, and I realized he was laughing.

Gruffy looked like he might take a nip at the toucan. "I am almost seven! And I will not stand by while injustice—"

"You're seven years old?" I asked.

"There are always injustices. Always injustices," Pip squawked. "And me and Squeak getting eaten by your father would be the largest! It would be the largest! The Eternal Sea is a million miles away. A million miles away." Pip flapped about, agitated. "And the Ink King is too strong. Too strong. Does anyone remember

the Tree Bender of Garrulous Grove? Of Garrulous Grove?"
Pip asked. "The Sky Captain? The Sky Captain? Even the Sand
Spinner has not been seen lately. Not seen lately. They crossed
the Ink King and now they're gone. Now they're gone."

Gruffy pointed a talon at Pip. "All the more reason—"

"What does he mean?" I asked. The Tree Bender and the Sky
Captain had to be Doolivantis. "What did the Ink King do?"

"You would take her right to him? Right to him?" Pip continued his tirade, ignoring me.

"I will protect her," Gruffy said.

"You can't even protect yourself. Protect yourself! The Ink
King had you bound and gagged. Bound and gagged."

Gruffy's lion tail lashed.

"Wait a minute!" I said, raising my voice. "What did he do
with them?"

"Squeak."

Both Pip and Gruffy looked at the little mouse as though he
had answered the question, then looked at me for my response.

I rolled my eyes. "I can't understand him!"

Gruffy bowed his head. "My apologies. The Ink King visited
them, and they vanished."

"He killed them?" I asked.

"He's powerful. Very powerful," Pip said.

"We don't know that for certain," Gruffy said.

"You're so concerned with being a hero that you'll put her in
danger! You'll put her in danger!" Pip said. "That's not what a
hero does. Not what a hero does."

"And my other choice is to let this villain win? I shall not!"
Gruffy said.

"That's not your responsibility. Not your responsibility! I'm going to your father. To your father."

Gruffy jumped into the air, his wings creating a mighty wind. Pip flew hastily out of his reach. The sudden gale pushed me back; I shielded my eyes.

"SQUEAK!"

Squeak stood on his hind legs, paws out like a miniature emperor.

"Squeak," he repeated, more quietly.

"We can't let him take her there," Pip protested. "We can't—"

"I'm going anyway," I interrupted. Everyone looked at me. "The Ink King has my family."

"You don't know that. Don't know that," Pip said.

"It's the only lead I have. For a whole year, I've had no explanation for why they vanished. No chance to bring them back. I've been told to 'move on.' But Veloran changes everything. What if they have been here for a whole year? I can't leave them trapped here with the Ink King. If there's even a chance I can save them, I'm going to the Eternal Sea."

Pip hovered, flicking his wings to keep himself aloft.

Gruffy landed, tucking his wings against his lion flanks.

"Squeak," said Squeak with finality.

"No one likes a know-it-all. Likes a know-it-all," Pip squawked peevishly.

Squeak smoothed his whiskers with his paws.

Ripple giggled, covering her mouth, and Gruffy made a clicking sound with his beak.

Pip's flapping became agitated, and he changed direction, flying back and forth.

"Well, I'll have to tell her, then. I'll have to tell her," he said, and took off toward the rising sun.

"Tell who?" I asked.

Gruffy, with that crook to his beak that I recognized as his smile, said, "His girlfriend."

"Oh!" I said, confused. "And how old is Pip?"

"About three. Which, to a human, would be about . . ." Gruffy thought.

"Squeak."

"Yes. About sixteen."

"And what about you? What would you be in human years?"

"I don't think age—" Gruffy began.

"Squeak."

Gruffy sighed. "About eleven, but griffons are different than humans in many—"

"Squeak."

Gruffy cleared his throat, trying to ignore whatever Squeak had said.

I went up to the griffon and punched him on the shoulder. He swiveled his head to look at me.

"Nothing wrong with being eleven." I said. "That makes us the same age."

Gruffy looked at me for a moment, then the corner of his beak curved up. "I did not mean to imply . . ." But he trailed off and looked over my shoulder.

I looked in the same direction and—

"Eeep!" I said.

"Well then," Gruffy said.

"Squeak," said Squeak.

An enormous, multicolored forest towered behind us, and it had *not* been there a second ago!

There were giant purple trees, long and thin. Their branches drooped to the ground. Behind them was a taller blue tree, and farther back, over the treetops, I could see orange leaves, red leaves, and silver leaves on other trees. My gaze returned to the edge of the forest and a clump of giant white flowers that were almost as tall as the purple trees.

"Phazing forests . . ." I breathed.

"That is the Kaleidoscope Forest, Doolivanti," Gruffy said.

"Yeah? How did it get here?"

"It is always there. It touches all parts of Veloran. That it is here is a good sign. It senses our need, as we must fly over it to reach the Eternal Sea."

"It moves where it wants to go?" I asked.

"No, Doolivanti. It touches all parts of Veloran. But sometimes you may see it. Sometimes you may not."

"Um, okay." That didn't make any sense at all.

"Now we must gather provisions, collect Pip, and return. Then we may begin our journey," Gruffy said. "But at least one of us must stay so the forest will remain."

"I'll do it," I said.

"I shall remain with thee," Ripple added.

Gruffy nodded. "Do not enter the forest. It is safe at this distance, but fraught with perils within. Squeak and I shall return shortly." Gruffy launched into the air and flapped out of sight.

I turned back to the forest and the giant white flowers. They were shaped like tulips. Their trunks were smooth and green and went straight up, separating into two other trunks, each bearing a giant white flower cup taller than I was. In between were shorter "trees." They looked like rumpled orange sweaters on green coils. I stepped closer, marveling, and I heard a chorus of tiny giggles. I stepped back, and they stopped.

I turned to Ripple. "Did you hear that?"

"Verily."

"Um, what?"

"I did."

"That's what 'verily' means?"

"Indeed, Lady Lorelei."

"So you were agreeing."

"Verily."

We both paused, then laughed.

"Apologies, my lady," Ripple said. "For thee, perchance I might say 'yes'?"

"No. I'll get it. My dad always said learning is a gift. Don't change the way you speak for me."

"Ah, a man of great wisdom, thy father?"

"Actually, he's a bit of a goof."

Ripple smiled gently.

I felt that dropping sensation in my stomach. Talking about Dad made me remember how much I missed him. I cleared my throat. "Anyway, you heard the giggles?" I asked instead.

"Verily." Ripple nodded and winked.

"Then verily where did they come from?" I said.

"I thought thou didst make them."

I stepped forward, and the giggles came again. Thin blades of grass curled gently around my purple shoes.

"Tis the grass," Ripple said.

I jumped back. "Did I hurt it?" I knelt down and ran my fingers over the short green blades. They wriggled, tickled my hand, and giggled again. I felt warm tingles from my fingers all the way to my heart.

"They're wonderful," I said. "It's like—"

A figure moved just beyond the giant white tulips, shaded by the thick trees, and I jumped to my feet. Sun flashed off something shiny, then the figure pulled back into the darkness.

"Did you see that?" I said, my heart thumping.

"Nay." Ripple followed my gaze. "'Twas a beast?"

"Something big. It might have had a sword or something metal."

"Prithee, keep thy distance."

I stepped forward, and the grasses giggled again. "Come out!" I said, but nothing moved. I went closer, nearing the first of the puffy orange sweater plants. I peered between the trunks, trying to spot the figure, but it was dark inside. Only a few paces into the forest, it was like the sun had gone out.

"Lady Lorelei . . ."

"I'm just going to—"

The orange sweater plant launched like a striking rattlesnake, wrapping around me. It was so fast I barely had time to turn. The orange "sleeves" were cool and soft, but strong. They yanked me deeper into the forest.

"Lady Lorelei!" Ripple started forward.

"No! Stay ba—"

The cup of a white tulip, towering over the patch of orange sweater plants, bent down and clapped its cup right on top of me. The sweater let go and the flower scooped me up. I sloshed around in thick water filled with things like coconuts. Above, the petals closed together almost completely, leaving an opening about the size of my head.

I clambered upright and jumped for it, grabbing the edges of the petals. They were firm, so I pulled up on them and poked my head out.

"Lady Lorelei! I am coming!" Ripple shouted, striding forward.

"No! Stay back. Don't let them get you, too."

"But thou art—"

"Just wait! There's no point in both of us getting swallowed."

"Thourt not hurt?"

"I'm okay. I mean, so far. There's some kind of water in here."

"Lady Lorelei, thourt the most intrepid maiden I've ever met."

I couldn't remember what intrepid meant. Dad had used it once. "I'm what? What am I?"

"Brave, my lady."

"Oh, good. Well, thanks." I looked around to find something that might—

Below, at the edge of the forest, a knight watched me. He wore armor so shiny, it looked like it was made out of mirrors. He was tall, his shoulders and arms exaggerated like a super-hero. Great spikes of mirrored metal poked up from his shoulder plates and out of his gauntlets. His face was only two mirrors angled to a point where his nose would have been. He sat upon a giant pug dog with reins in its stumpy mouth. The pug's eyes were also mirrors, glinting in the bright light, and it seemed to be looking at nothing.

"Ripple! Watch out!" I shouted.

The knight stayed a moment longer, then wheeled the pug around and dove back into the dark forest.

"Ripple, did you—"

"Verily! A man of mirrors!"

"A knight!"

"A what?" Ripple asked.

I craned my chin over the lip of the flower petal. "Ripple, you speak like Shakespeare in the Park, but you don't know what a knight is?"

"Do they swim?"

I laughed. After a moment, I let out a breath and dropped back down into the bowl created by the flower petals. My arms were starting to hurt. "I need to get out of here," I shouted out to Ripple.

"Art thou in distress?"

"Um, no." The coconut things knocked against my shoes and stuck. "Not yet." I shook one off, and it splashed into the ankle-deep water, which was thicker now. I picked one up. It was brown and oval and looked like a seed. And it was sticky. I had to shake it to get it off my hand.

"There are seeds in here!"

The flower suddenly moved, and I fell against the side of the bowl.

"Lady Lorelei!" Ripple cried.

The water sloshed over me, and the seeds stuck to my arms and legs and chest and back. The petals undulated from the bottom of the bowl, squeezing upward. The flower tipped and spat me out.

I spun across the grass in an eddy of sludgy goop, and the

grass giggled. A few seeds twisted off as I tumbled, but most of them stuck.

Ripple hurried to my side. "Art thou injured?"

I stood up, covered in seeds and goop. "Ripple, did this flower spit all over me? Did I just get barfed up by a flower?"

Ripple giggled, putting a delicate blue hand over her mouth. The grass giggled with her.

I stood up, knocking off the sticky seeds. They were very reluctant to let go.

"Ho, Doolivanti!"

Gruffy and Pip flapped down from the sky. Squeak was riding atop Gruffy's head, as usual.

"Squeak!"

"I guess she did. I guess she did," Pip squawked.

I shook out my hands, flicking tulip snot onto the ground. Pip flapped backward out of the spray. Gruffy landed next to me, seeming not to notice the flecks that landed on him.

"Ew," I said. "Just ew."

"I should have warned you," Gruffy said. "Everyone knows about the Tasting Tulips. But neither of you are from here."

"Do they ever swallow people? I mean, like, digest them?" I asked.

Gruff clicked his beak. "No, Doolivanti. This is how they spread their seeds. They pick up a passing creature, cover it in seeds, and let the creature run away with the seeds attached to them. The creature will eventually clean them off somewhere, and more Tasting Tulips can grow. But the tulips are harmless."

"I was just used as a human bee?" Mom called me "Lori-bee." Sometimes just "My little bee." Now I really was!

Gruffy cocked his head. "What is a bee?"

"You don't have bees?"

"Perhaps in other places on Veloran. What is it?"

"A bug that flies. It has black and yellow stripes, and it carries pollen between flowers so that they can grow more flowers."

Gruffy's feather brow furrowed. "Truly? How could a bug carry seeds of this size?"

"They don't . . . It's not . . ." I shook my head. "Never mind."

"Well, if you are ready, we now have food. Shall we go?"

"Please."

I took off my jean jacket and wrung it out.

"I don't suppose you brought a towel?" I asked.

"What's a towel? What's a towel?" Pip squawked.

"Never mind."

CHAPTER *12*

GRUFFY LOWERED A WING AND I EAGERLY GOT ON HIS BACK.

"Sweet!" I said.

Ripple, though, looked less than thrilled. "Fly?"

"Come on, Ripple. It'll be just like swimming," I said. "Except through the air!"

"I shall not let you fall," Gruffy said.

The princess hesitated. I extended a hand. After a moment, she took it and I helped her up.

"Hang on tight," I said.

"Twill have my most fervent attention, I assure thee," Ripple replied, squeezing my waist tightly.

Gruffy leapt into the air.

Ripple screamed and practically squeezed my guts out. I gasped, then laughed, trying to catch my breath. I looked down and could see everything, from the desert around Azure City to Urath's rocky ravine. It was like being in an airplane, except the wind was all around me.

"Tis not like swimming," Ripple said, clinging tightly, her head pressed against my back. "Not in the slightest."

"I shall not let you fall," Gruffy repeated.

I reveled in the rushing air. The forest below was a riot of color. In Colorado, forests were firs and spruce, all dark green and uniform, with the occasional patch of light green aspen clusters. This looked like a painter's palette: some green, but also bursts of red and purple and yellow and silver. Thick stalks with no branches rose up like Greek columns, fat leaves growing straight out of the trunk. Slender silver trees rose above the canopy of the forest on lacework trunks, branches arcing out over the top of everything else. Their leaves glinted like silver coins and they seemed so fragile that the wind might shatter them.

There were also black-limbed trees, looking like they had been burnt. Their sinuous limbs shifted back and forth as though testing the air, seeking something. Each black tree stood in its own clearing; the other trees kept their distance.

And some weren't even trees, like the Tasting Tulips. They were something else, either giant flowers or, in some cases animals who were trying to look like trees. One of the animals had to be as tall as a two-story building. Its back was leafy and purple, but it was no tree. It was shaped like a giant horse.

The forest captivated me. The princess and I just stared and stared.

But after a few hours, I started shifting one way and then another, trying to find a spot I could sit that didn't make my butt numb. Gruffy's back was so feathery and soft at first, but now it seemed all backbone. I looked over my shoulder at Ripple, who rode in silence. The princess was much better at hiding her discomfort than I was. I shifted again, looked up at the sky. The fiery red line I had seen last night was still there. It was ugly and mean-looking.

"Are we landing soon?" I asked.

"My wings are beat. My wings are beat," Pip squawked.

I looked at Squeak for his inevitable "squeak" that I couldn't understand, but the little mouse's gaze was fixed below.

"A rest would be prudent," Gruffy conceded.

"How much longer until we reach the sea?"

"Another full day of flying," Gruffy said, and then, "There. That looks like a good spot." He indicated with his claw one of the clearings that held a shifting black tree.

"That's where you want to land? That's where you want to land?" Pip said dubiously.

"I must have space. If I dive straight down through those branches, it would strip my noble passengers right off my back." He nodded at me and Ripple.

"Squeak."

"I shall be careful, my friend."

"I agree with Squeak," I said. I didn't understand the mouse, but I got the gist: black trees were bad news. If the rest of the forest kept clear, we should, too.

"I shall land outside its reach. Will that suffice?" Gruffy asked.

We swooped low, and as we neared, Ripple's grasp on my waist tightened. We landed at the edge of the clearing around the black tree. I kept my eyes on the thing, but it just waved its sooty branches back and forth, side to side.

It reminded me of the octopus shadow from the camping trip.

"How are you faring, Doolivanti? Princess?" Gruffy asked as we dismounted.

"Thourt a prince of the air," Ripple said. "A creature of unfailing strength and courtesy." She took a half-step back and dipped into a curtsey, lifting the hem of her sparkling blue gown and spreading it to the side like a jeweled wing. She inclined her head.

"Well, it was nothing any griffon would not do." He cleared his throat. "Please," he reached back with his beak and undid the pack strapped around his middle. "You must be hungry. There is plenty of food."

We sat down on the sparse grass at the edge of the clearing and opened the pack. It was full of different pouches: a skin of water, seeds and nuts, a big bag of bright green apples, and scaly orange egg things. They were about the size of a chicken's egg, and just as hard. I tapped one with my fingernail, and it clicked like a countertop.

"What's this?"

Pip cocked his head toward me. "It's a goolaroose. A goolaroose."

"How do you eat it?"

"Ah," Gruffy said. "The goolaroose is most pleasing." He took one and tapped his talon hard against it. The scaly surface cracked, and a bright red, feathery sprig billowed up out of the crack, growing quickly. Gruffy put it to his beak and scraped the feathery thing into his mouth.

"Wow!" I looked at the egg, then cracked it on a little rock next to me. The sprig rose out of the crack like a curl of red smoke. I held it at arm's length.

"Quickly! Quickly!" Pip squawked.

"But, it's growing!" I said. "Is it going to keep growing inside my mouth?"

But even as I spoke, the little sprig stopped growing at about the width of my hand, and then faded to yellow. The feathery fronds shrank. It turned brown, then gray. The feather became brittle then burst into a puff of dust.

"Goolaroose gone bad. Goolaroose gone bad." Pip shook his head, let out a little breath. "So sad. So sad."

"I'm sorry!"

Gruffy chuckled. "It's Pip's favorite fruit, in case you could not tell." He tossed me another and I caught it. "Try again. This time a little quicker." He winked.

I cracked the fruit again, and this time, I immediately put the billowing fruit in my mouth. Sweet and lime and a touch of spice spread across my tongue.

"Flippin fluffy feathers," I murmured around the dancing flavors in my mouth. "It's womderfuw!"

"Best taste in all of Veloran. In all of Veloran." Pip deftly cracked a goolaroose on the edge of his beak and scooped out the feathery sprig.

The princess tried next, and squeaked with delight. We all set to eating. As I munched on some of the nuts that Pip called "bahamaknockanuts"—which looked like blue almonds and tasted like chocolate cake—I noticed Squeak had not joined us for the feast. I spotted him halfway toward the black tree. He would scurry forward, lift his nose to the air, then scurry forward some more.

"Gruffy," I warned.

Gruffy looked over at Squeak, then back at me, unworried. "Squeak is always curious." Not for the first time, I regretted that I couldn't understand the little mouse when everyone else could.

"Aren't you afraid he might get hurt?" I asked.

"By what?"

"That tree."

Gruffy looked at the tree, then back at me. "Squeak is quite fast."

Jimmy was right about Gruffy. He was not curious about the world. Pip was the same way. But Squeak, perhaps, was not.

I looked the other way, into the deep dark of the forest. It seemed so peaceful. When I finished eating, I got up to explore a little. Pip and Ripple were talking about the coastline of the Eternal Sea, and Gruffy had begun to preen his feathers again.

I walked into the forest. It was darker in the shade of the trees, and I spotted some little golden fruits underneath a gnarled bush in the shadows. The bush's limbs were curled and covered with thorns of all sizes. Some were tiny as hairs, and others were long as my pinky finger. The golden fruits, full-to-bursting and shaped like peaches, nestled among the thorns.

They glinted, and I couldn't tell whether the fruits were glowing, or catching some ray of light I couldn't see.

They seemed so right, to pluck and . . . not eat. No, not that. But to hold. To keep close.

I approached the bush and, carefully avoiding the thorns, plucked one. It came off easily in my hand, and it was fuzzy all over. I stroked the light fur and turned it over. It felt good; it felt right—

"So you messed with the Starfield," a soft voice came from the shadows.

I jumped, clutching the golden fruit so tight my fingers sank into it. "Jimmy!"

Except it wasn't just Jimmy. It was Jimmy and . . . something else. His face seemed to darken, as though a cloud had passed overhead.

"What's on your face?" I asked.

"You're such a cheater. You break all the rules." He shook his head, and I could hear the anger in his voice. Shadows slithered over his face and hands. He balled his hand into a fist. "You don't belong here."

He had sent me to the Starfield. He knew what it would do, what it almost *had* done before I made it stop.

"You tried to kill me!" I said.

The shadows covered him completely, and black tentacles grew out of his sides. "This is your last chance, Loreliar. Leave the Wishing World, and I won't hurt you or your *friends*."

The shadows on his body were the same ones that had reached over my tent on that rainy night my family vanished. "It was you! You took them! You're the Ink King."

"They are the parents I should have had. The kind who come to school even to see you *lose* a stupid spelling bee. I should have had them, not you. And now I do."

I couldn't catch my breath. Jimmy had used the Wishing World to steal my brother, my parents! I squeezed the fruit so hard it should have been crushed. But as my fingers dug in I felt the firmness of the center, like there was a sphere of steel inside.

"You know how many times my dad came to the school to watch me at anything?" Jimmy asked. He held up a hand and made a zero. "None. Never."

"You . . ." I managed to say in a breathless tone, "can't just do that."

He smiled, oily black skin next to white teeth. "In the Wishing World, I do whatever I want. Here, I'm the strongest Doolivanti ever."

I thought about what Gruffy had said, about the Ink King removing other Doolivantis. Even killing them. The Sky Captain. The Tree Bender. Maybe the Sand Spinner, too.

"There were other kids from Earth, weren't there?"

"Go home, Loreliar. I'm warning you. Go home or you'll wish you had."

"Give my parents back!" I shouted.

"Stupid girl," Jimmy said. "You always were a stupid girl." He waved a hand.

"Squeak!"

I heard Squeak's cry and spun, looking back through the forest. Gruffy stood in a brilliant opening of light, bordered by leafy limbs and bushes. I was much deeper into the forest than I'd realized.

"Doolivanti!" Gruffy called, not seeing me. Ripple was already on his back, ready to fly, and behind him dozens of giant roaches swarmed down the black tree. They were as big as dogs and the color of burnt butter. Squeak darted across the meadow, a gray streak of light, and he leapt onto Gruffy's head.

The roaches sprang onto the clearing. They glistened like they were wet, and their feet were hooked claws that tore up the ground. Yellow eyes glowed in their tiny heads.

"Doolivanti!" Gruffy called. He growled in frustration, then leapt powerfully into the air, flattening Ripple against his back. The roaches hissed at the suddenly flying griffon. The nearest jumped like a giant flea and sank its hooks into Gruffy's side, but he ripped it off with his beak and spat it down at the rest.

"Nay! We cannot leave her!" Ripple said.

"She might have gone through one of her portals," Gruffy said. "I must get you to safety first." The roaches scaled the trees, reaching Gruffy's height and jumping at him. He batted one to the ground, beat his wings backward and batted another down with his lion legs.

I watched them as I clutched the golden fruit, and I let out a low growl. They were leaving me! My friends!

The golden fruit purred.

Whatever. I didn't need Gruffy. I didn't need any of them. Jimmy had my family. That was all that mattered.

I turned back to him, but Jimmy was gone.

"Show yourself!" I shouted.

The sallow roaches clicked and turned toward my shout, seeing me for the first time. They sprang from the tree and scuttled toward me, hissing.

What the heck was I doing?

With a shriek, I turned and sprinted.

"Gruffy!" I shouted, pushing through the forest. Bushes tore at my jeans. Thin limbs slapped my face. "Gruffy!" I shouted.

"Doolivanti!"

I heard his voice somewhere above the darkness of the tight, leafy canopy.

The roaches were right behind me. One of them hissed next to my ear.

Tree limbs cracked like thunder, and bright light burst into the forest as Gruffy tore through the canopy. His wings flared and he landed like a falling bomb, screeching at the roaches.

The foul bugs pulled up short, clicking and hissing. They spread out in a circle around us, rustling through the grass.

"Quickly, Doolivanti," Gruffy urged.

I clutched the golden fruit to my chest, squeezing it until I could feel that satisfying hardness underneath.

"Where were you when I needed you?!" I demanded. "You left me!"

"Doolivanti—" Gruffy looked at me, surprised and confused. "We must fly now—"

But there was no more time.

The roaches leapt upon us.

CHAPTER *13*

A GIANT ROACH FLATTENED ME AND I HIT THE GROUND HARD. Its hooked feet poked into my back, and I screamed.

Then Gruffy's strong talon was there, yanking me upright and batting the roach aside. He tucked me underneath his feathery, furry belly, unfurling his wings and settling them protectively on either side.

I could see the roaches through his front legs, circling again. They wanted me, the small one, not the giant griffon. I tried to still my chattering teeth and clutched the golden fruit even harder.

"I cannot fight them all and keep you safe." Gruffy uncurled his talon. "We must flee." He grabbed me around the middle and leapt straight up.

But the roaches were ready this time. Many of them had already climbed into the nearby trees and leapt onto Gruffy's back. He screeched and fought them, but for every roach he snatched away with his beak, three more jumped on him.

He faltered, his wings straining. He canted sideways and hit a tree, struggling to flap, trying to catch the air, but he was tangled in branches and covered in roaches. He screeched, clawing against the trunk to shove himself upward. The roach nearest me opened its mouth, revealing two pointed pincers, and sank them into Gruffy's arm. Gruffy's talon spasmed and he dropped me.

I tumbled through the branches, smacking each harder than the last, and landed on the ground with a thud. The golden fruit rolled across the forest floor.

Gruffy hurtled sideways, trying to fight two dozen roaches that covered him. He crashed into the trees and was borne to the ground under the swarming attack. Gruffy fought them, but he was losing. They were biting him so many times!

"Gruffy!" I screamed.

Roaches dropped to the ground all around me. I spun about. Yellow eyes and pincers clicked everywhere I turned. They closed on me, hissing.

Doolivanti, I thought. *I am a Doolivanti. I broke a wall. I can stop these bugs.*

I could make a wall of my own, block them out. I could—

Behind me, undergrowth burst open and a flash of light charged into the clearing. It was the mirror knight from the edge of the forest! He was the tallest man I'd ever seen, with wide shoulders and a round shield on his arm.

The giant pug he rode churned the earth with its paws. Atop the pug's wide head rode Squeak.

"Squeak squeak!" Squeak leapt to the ground.

The pug's smooshed face opened and he gave a thunderous bark as he stepped on the nearest roach, squishing it with a loud *snap*. The knight leapt to the ground and charged the roaches on Gruffy, bashing three of them away with one sweep of his shield. He smacked another with his fist, sending it hurtling into the bushes.

The pug lunged at the roaches surrounding me, barking and snapping and scattering them in every direction.

Between the ferocious griffon, the giant pug, and the knight, the roaches had had enough. They fled, and the battle was over that quickly.

"Gruffy!" I shouted, running to the griffon and throwing my arms around his neck. "I'm so sorry!"

"It is all right, Doolivanti," Gruffy said.

There was blood on his fur. "They hurt you."

"Not as much as we hurt them." He inclined his head to the knight, who stood silently a few feet away. "Thanks to you, friend."

The knight nodded, and the giant pug padded up behind him, his enormous head towering over all of them. Squeak dashed across the forest floor and stopped in front of Gruffy.

"Squeak." Squeak's whiskers twitched.

"You were quite resourceful," Gruffy said, nodding, and there was admiration in his voice. "When I asked you to find help, I only hoped you might find the Mirror Man in time."

"Squeak."

"Ah!" Gruffy laughed. "Then fate was on our side."

"What did he say?" I asked.

Gruffy nodded at the knight. "This mighty warrior has no name that we have ever heard. He never speaks. He never ventures past the boundaries of the Kaleidoscope Forest, and he and his giant friend protect all who are in danger here. Those who know of him call him the Mirror Man."

"I saw him at the edge of the forest, right after I was swallowed by the Tasting Tulip."

"Ah," Gruffy said. "He was waiting, no doubt, to see if you would come to harm."

I walked up to the knight, who stood completely still. I couldn't shake a sense of familiarity.

"Do I know you?" I asked, peering up at my own face in the refection of his mirrored helmet.

"He never speaks, Doolivanti," Gruffy said. "The legends say he silently does his duty and goes on his way."

"Squeak."

I wanted to reach up and touch that helmet. There were no eye slits or breathing holes. "Do you have a name?" I asked.

The knight said nothing.

"Thank you." I reached up and touched the center of his shield. When in my life had I ever known a knight? I ached to push back his visor and see his face.

I noticed a flash of gold in his hand behind the shield. I tilted my head to see better. He was holding a golden fruit just like the one I'd found before the roaches attacked.

"Thank you," I repeated.

"Darthorn," the knight said.

"What?"

"Squeak!"

"I . . . am . . . Darthorn," the knight said.

"Remarkable," said Gruffy.

"Do I know you, Darthorn?" I asked.

The knight stepped away, took two strides, and leapt upon the back of the pug, who raised his head and snuffled, shaking his neck at the weight of the Mirror Man. The pug wheeled around and dove into the forest.

Darthorn was gone.

"I have never heard of the Mirror Man talking to anyone," Gruffy said. "You are truly unique, Doolivanti."

"I know him," I whispered.

"You do?"

"From somewhere. I don't know where."

Gruffy looked at the now-quiet forest where the knight had disappeared.

I tried to piece it together. So much had happened that my mind was spinning. There was something about the knight, something I couldn't put my finger on. It niggled at me like a sliver underneath my skin.

I went back to the tree where I had fallen.

"We must return to the princess and Pip, Doolivanti," Gruffy said.

"Just a second." I picked up the golden fruit. "I was missing this." My fingers sank into the soft surface, felt the hardness beneath. Yes, that was better. I felt bigger, stronger.

"Where did you get that?" Gruffy asked.

"Squeak!"

"A bush by the clearing with the black tree." I didn't like the way he had asked that question. "Why?"

"'Tis a Grudge, Doolivanti. You'll want—"

"Don't tell me what I want," I snapped, holding the fruit away from them. "You have no idea what I want." I took a step back.

"Squeak." The little mouse shook his paws out like there was something sticky on them.

"Indeed it has," Gruffy said to Squeak, then to me. "Your scant knowledge of Veloran works against you, Doolivanti. You should not hold a Grudge."

"I'll hold what I want, griffon." I looked down at my fist, white knuckles tight over the spongy surface of the golden fruit.

Gruffy clicked his beak and looked at Squeak, then back at me. "'Tis dangerous, Doolivanti."

"Well, whose fault is that, then?" I demanded. "You made us land by that black tree. If we hadn't, I wouldn't have gone into the forest. Those horrible bugs wouldn't have chased us! You wouldn't have gotten cut all over by their claws. It's your fault. Don't blame me!"

"No one blames you, Doolivanti." Gruffy's voice was very calm now. "We care about your welfare. Would you loan me the Grudge for only a moment?"

"It's mine!"

"Just for a moment."

"I don't trust you, griffon. And why should I—"

In the middle of my sentence, Squeak became a gray blur,

streaking up my arm. He snatched the fruit and leapt away. The fruit writhed in Squeak's teeth, coming alive. Beady little black eyes and ratlike fangs appeared in the golden, fuzzy hide. Squeak flung it away. It unfurled—larger than the charcoal mouse—and chattered angrily.

I gasped, and the sense of strength fled, replaced by a cold shame. I drew a breath at the horrible things I had said.

"Oh my gosh! I'm so sorry!"

The Grudge charged Squeak, fangs bared. Squeak jumped up, bounced on its back, and landed on the far side. He then stood on his hind legs and did a victory dance.

"Squeak!"

The Grudge charged again, hissing and spitting, awkward little feet scuttling across the ground. Squeak dodged and smacked it on the backside.

"Squeak!"

"Is he saying 'Olé!'?" I whispered to Gruffy.

Gruffy looked at me. "What is Olé?"

I sighed. "Never mind."

The Grudge snapped and clawed and kicked at Squeak all at once, but it missed and tripped over its own legs, wadding itself up into a golden ball. It unfurled and looked at the mouse, who clapped his paws together twice and waited.

The Grudge chittered in fury, turned, and plunged into the undergrowth, but not before Squeak spun, slapping the Grudge's backside with his tail.

Squeak stared after it to be sure it was gone, then turned and scampered back to Gruffy.

"Well done, Squeak," Gruffy acknowledged. Squeak merely nodded once and hopped up onto Gruffy's head.

"That thing was making me angry," I said, understanding now. "It was controlling my emotions!"

"That is what a Grudge does," Gruffy said. "The longer you hold one, the angrier you get, until that is all you can see. You soon forget who your friends are. You can even forget your own safety."

"It was like I was someone else. I didn't even—" I gasped, turning in the direction the Mirror Man, Darthorn, had gone. "Darthorn had one. He had a Grudge."

"Squeak?"

"Are you certain? I saw nothing," Gruffy said.

"It was in his hand behind the shield. It looked like his fingers were sunk into it." I looked at them. "We have to find him! Help him!"

"Squeak."

"I'm sorry, Doolivanti, but Squeak is right. Pip and the princess await us. We left them most precariously perched atop a Silverweft tree. If the roaches find them, they might climb the tree to get them. We cannot wait any longer."

I bit my lip, staring into the forest where the knight had gone. "Can we look for him afterward?"

"We may try, but the Mirror Man appears where he will. We may not be able to find him," Gruffy said. "However, should we need him again, I have little doubt he will reappear."

"Why?" I asked.

"Because that is what the Mirror Man does."

"Darthorn," I murmured, trying again to fit the name to some memory. I couldn't. With a sigh, I climbed onto Gruffy. He leapt into the air and flapped through the giant hole he had made in the forest's ceiling.

CHAPTER 14

WE PICKED UP RIPPLE AND PIP AND CONTINUED ON, FLYING over the forest. We looked for the giant pug and his rider, but as Gruffy suspected, the Mirror Man had vanished.

My chest felt empty. Gruffy told me that releasing a Grudge caused such emptiness, but I knew it had more to do with Darthorn. I had held a Grudge for only a few minutes, and it had made me so angry that I'd run away from my friends when they were only trying to help. What would it do to poor Darthorn, who might have been holding it much longer?

We flew for the remainder of the day, and as the sun set, Gruffy began looking for a good place to camp.

"How about a nice big clearing with a black tree? A black tree," Pip squawked.

Gruffy took a playful snap at the toucan, who flapped backward.

It was Squeak who picked the location, a happy little glade with chest-high green ferns and a babbling brook for Ripple that splashed over clusters of rocks and glinted orange in the setting sun. Gruffy landed and we all stretched our legs.

"'Tis not my strength, riding griffons," Ripple admitted, twisting to the left and then to the right, hands on her hips. She then stepped into the water and sighed as she sat down. "'Twill be nary a moment and I shall emerge. Prithee, feel not obliged to await my return ere thou dost break bread," she said, then laid down and let the stream cover her whole body.

We waited for her anyway, and when she emerged, we all sat down and ate more goolaroose, green apples, and nuts. Squeak said that he would take the night watch, or so I gathered. He claimed that he had slept peacefully atop Gruffy's head during the flight, and was refreshed.

Pip found a branch overhead and tucked his beak under one wing. I looked for a good place to lie down, but Gruffy cleared his throat and bowed his head to me. "Doolivanti, I would have a word with you, if I may."

"Of course," I said.

Gruffy walked away from Pip, Ripple, and Squeak, far enough that he could not be overheard. He seemed uncomfortable.

"Are you okay?" I asked.

He cleared his throat. "Doolivanti, I understand that you are powerful. I would never question this. You are a wish maker, but . . ." He hesitated.

"Gruffy, we're friends. You can tell me. What is it?"

"I would not normally presume so far, but there is so much you do not seem to know about Veloran. It is twice now that I have almost lost you. A Doolivanti! You did not know about the danger of the Starfield. You did not know about the Grudge. You went too far into the Kaleidoscope Forest. And though every time you have managed to come out safely, they were all very near escapes. I have failed to protect you adequately."

"Gruffy, you were amazing," I said. "You saved my life."

"You are too kind." He bowed his head. "But I would like to give you something, if I may." He turned his head and put his beak gently over his snowy mane of feathers. He plucked a feather free and dropped it into my hand.

The snow-white feather was one of his smaller ones, but it was nearly as long as my forearm. It was warm to the touch.

"Griffons do not molt like birds, Doolivanti," Gruffy continued. "Did you know that?"

"No."

"Only by force might we lose our feathers. They are part of us. Like my talons. Or my eyes. I may, however, give a single feather to a friend."

"Gruffy, you don't have to—"

He shook his head, and I stopped talking.

"This feather belongs to you," he said. "It is yours. You may choose not to accept it, which I would understand—"

"Of course I accept it!"

He sighed in relief. "Thank you. You honor me, Doolivanti."

"Gruffy," I stammered, looking at the amazing gift. It seemed to glow in the moonlight. "I-I don't know what to say."

"There is more to it," he said. "This feather is connected to me, and if you wear it, you will be, too. If you are in need and your slightest breath touches the feather, I will know it, and I will be able to find you."

"I blow on it and you can find me?"

"The wind is the companion of the griffon. The wind you create is even more precious to me. If we are ever separated again, you need only call. I will answer."

"Gruffy . . ."

"I will protect you, Doolivanti. None shall harm you so long as I breathe. I swear it."

I threw my arms around his neck and hugged him tight. After a moment, he brought a taloned arm up and wrapped it around me.

"Thank you, Gruffy. I'll wear it always."

"Thank *you*, Doolivanti."

My mind swirled with so many thoughts, but I held the feather tightly as we returned to the clearing. Ripple's eyes widened when she saw it, but she didn't say anything. Squeak also watched me, his dark little eyes flicking from the snow-white feather to my face and back again. He, too, made no comment. Pip was asleep.

Gruffy laid down, and Ripple and I snuggled against his furry, feathery hide. I fell asleep holding Gruffy's feather tightly.

My dreams were colorful and without sense. The faces of

Mr. Schmindly and Tabitha flashed by. A worried Auntie Carrie and Uncle Jone, talking to policemen at my house. I saw Mom and Dad behind the shadowy bars of a prison. I saw my brother running through a forest, holding the stone knight that Dad gave him, his wavy golden hair bouncing atop his head.

I woke, and sat up. Gruffy's chest rose and fell in slumber. Ripple was curled into his side, the stars in her hair glowing softly. Her long gown looked like a river that had suddenly stopped moving. On a branch above, Pip sat immobile, beak tucked under his wing.

I stood up, and turned. He was nearby. The Mirror Man. Darthorn. I could feel the connection between us. I peered into the forest, searching.

Just beyond the stream in the shadows, I saw his tall silhouette astride the giant pug.

Scritch scratch.

I looked down. Squeak stood at my shoe. He looked up with his tiny, marble-like eyes.

"Please don't wake the others," I said, glancing back at Darthorn. "I . . . need to talk to him."

Squeak looked at the Mirror Man, then back at me. He smoothed his whiskers on both sides of his face, then sat down.

"I'll be okay." I jumped across the brook and moved toward the towering Mirror Man, who slowly dismounted the pug and waited.

"Darthorn," I said.

He stood absolutely still.

"I know you. And you know me, don't you?" I walked up to him, touched the big shield on his left arm, then moved my fingers to the edge and pulled it open, revealing his fist, clutched tight around the golden Grudge.

I put my fingers over his.

"I want you to give this to me," I said.

He moved his hand away from mine.

"You've held it a long time—" I began, but the catch in my throat stopped me.

I suddenly knew who he was, who he had to be.

He and his giant friend protect all who are in danger . . .

"I want you to show me who you were before you touched this," I said.

He didn't move for a long time. Then, slowly, the mirrored fingers separated, and he opened his hand. I batted the Grudge aside. Darthorn flinched, his helmeted head swiveling to look at it.

I kept his giant mirrored hand in mine until his head swiveled back to look down at me.

"It's okay," I said. My reflection in his helmet was tall and warped. "We'll figure it out together. I promise."

For a long moment, Darthorn simply stood there, unmoving. Then, suddenly, his armor began to slide aside in pieces the size of playing cards. Square upon square of mirror slid back, joining with the next square, and then the next. The mirrors retreated all over his body, receding like a wave up to his helmet, and then down to his shield. The shield went last, shrinking until all of the pieces became one card-sized mirror that he held in the same hand that had held the Grudge.

Darthorn was taller than any adult I'd ever met. His muscular shoulders, arms, and torso were mighty. Nobody was that muscular, except in comic books. He had wavy gold hair and a strong jaw. I knew his face, though it was the face of a man and not the little boy my brother had been.

"Theron . . ."

"Darthorn." He shook his head.

He had the same gray eyes, the wide nose. This was my brother. Even at nine years old, he'd always had wide shoulders and a strong body. Theron could climb up doorjambs and hang from them by his fingertips. He was constantly moving, playing, sprinting, jumping, wrestling. If Theron had become one of his own superheroes, this was what he would look like.

"Theron . . ." I tried to keep my voice steady. "It's me, Lorelei."

"I am Darthorn."

The name he had chosen confirmed it, which was why it had stuck in my mind from the start. Theron and I used to invent fictional characters together and draw them, play them out. Theron always drew superheroes. When he was four years old, his most powerful superhero was Thorn Boy. Thorn Boy could defeat Superman, the Hulk. He could wrap Spider-Man into a ball. But as Theron grew older, he made superheroes stronger than Thorn Boy. Superheroes who sounded more like men. But they always had the word "thorn" in them. Megathorn. Killthorn. Thornbomb.

Darthorn.

"Theron, it's me, Lorelei," I repeated.

"I . . ." he said.

I took his hands. It was so strange to look up at this man I knew wasn't a man. His fingers were powerful, strapped with tendons, not the pudgy fingers of a boy.

"I missed you," I said. "I didn't know where you went. I was all alone."

"I . . . can't be Theron," the man said.

"You can."

"No."

"You *are* Theron—"

"Theron can't . . ."

He trailed off, and I searched his face. But he looked over my head, as though he was concentrating on something far away.

"What can't Theron do?"

"He can't . . . save Dad."

I hugged him around the waist, as tightly as I could.

Darthorn began to shrink. In moments, he was my size, then shorter, then the size the nine-year-old Theron had been when he disappeared in the woods.

He fell to his knees and I went with him. "I couldn't save him," Theron said, crumpling into me. "I was a coward."

I held him as I used to do after one of his nightmares. It was just like it used to be, except larger. This time, he hadn't saved me from Shandra or Danny Brogue or even mean Mrs. Coswell. He'd saved me from real monsters. Larger-than-life roaches. And I could hold him. That much, I could do.

"I ran away . . ." Theron said. "It was attacking Dad, and I ran. I shouldn't have run. I let the monster get him."

"Tell me from the beginning."

"I wish I'd never gone to the outhouse," he mumbled. He let me go and turned toward the brook, wrapped his arms around his knees. He looked at the water and his voice became a monotone.

"The clouds were heavy," he said. "There were no stars. I knew it was going to rain, but I really had to go. So Dad took me."

"I remember," I said.

"So we went to the outhouse and I used it and then we went back outside. There was already thunder." He opened his hand, and the mirrored playing card had become the silvery stone knight figurine Dad had given him, nestled in his palm. "I left it in the outhouse," he said, looking at the figure. "I set it down and left it there by accident. And then when we were almost back to the tent, I remembered. I told Dad we had to go back, but he said it would be there in the morning and we could get it then. So I . . . I yanked my hand out of his and ran back to the outhouse."

He paused.

"I should have waited until morning. I should have listened to him. But I didn't." He turned the figure over in his hand. "When I came out of the outhouse, there was a monster. A real monster, not like we used to make up. It was on Dad's head, an octopus with black tentacles. Dad was fighting, but it was winning, and I . . ."

He slammed his fists against his head.

"Theron, don't—"

"I ran, Lore. I was so scared. I didn't know what to do. I didn't know monsters were really real. So I ran." He shook his head. "I should have fought it, but I ran."

I scooted next to him and put my arm around him. "You did what you were supposed to do. If Dad couldn't fight it, you couldn't have."

He shook his head. "Well, I turned around. When I stopped

being so scared, I ran back to fight the monster. I knew I wasn't big enough, but I wished for it so hard that I heard a voice whispering that I could be. That I could be Darthorn. And I started to feel bigger. But I couldn't find Dad. All the trees were different. They weren't the campground trees anymore, they were these trees." He waved at the forest around him. "I couldn't find him, and I swore that no one else would get attacked if I could help it. And I forgot about the campground. I forgot about you and Mom and Dad. I didn't mean to."

I put a hand on his arm.

"Where is the campground?" he asked. "How did I lose it?"

"It's not here," I said. "This isn't our world."

He looked back at his silver figure in his hand. "Where are we?"

"Gruffy calls it Veloran."

"Have you been here all this time, too?"

"No," I said. "I was left behind. I've been living with Auntie Carrie and Uncle Jone. For a whole year. But Dad's stone brought me here." I pulled the necklace out. "I wished to find you guys, and I came here."

"You wished?"

"Yes. I can make things happen. Like you made yourself into Darthorn. And I know who took Mom and Dad."

"You do?" he asked, looking up at me. His stone knight flattened into the mirrored card and unfolded over his hand, then unfolded again, starting to cover his arm.

"Wait," I said. "He's not here. He's taken Ripple's kingdom, and that's where we're going. His name is Jimmy. A boy from our world."

Theron narrowed his eyes. "Jimmy who?"

"He was in Annalee's class. Short red hair."

Theron's face darkened. "I know that boy. He beat up Micah." He clenched his teeth. "He's a bully." His mouth became a flat line and he looked at me through narrowed eyes. "Jimmy Schmindly."

My ears rang. "What?" I whispered. Mr. Schmindly. *Have you seen my son?* Mr. Schmindly's son *was* the Ink King!

"I don't forget names," Theron said, mistaking my question for disbelief. "And it's a doofy last name."

The Ink King's father was my praying mantis shrink, who knew about the Wishing World, who had been trying to control me for almost a year now. I could barely breathe. I felt like I'd eaten rotten food.

"He has our parents?" Theron asked.

"Yes," I said. Mr. Schmindly. Jimmy Schmindly. Froggy Pop Star Schmindly. All working together.

"Well, he's going to give them back," Theron growled.

"Yes," I said. "Yes, he is."

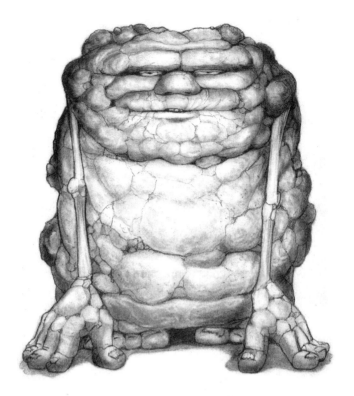

CHAPTER I5

MY BROTHER AND I LAY ON THE BANK OF THE STREAM WITH
our feet in the cool water. We stared up at the white streaks of
the night sky, barely able to see the "blue moon" beyond.

"That's Earth," I told him. "That's our home."

"We're on the comet?"

"Yes."

"Dad would think that's so cool."

"Yeah, he would."

Without my family, I had always felt like I was falling, like there was no real ground to stand on. But I had Theron back now. Anything was possible. As long as we had each other, we could get our parents back, no matter how many Ink Kings or Mantis Doctors tried to stop us.

I didn't remember falling back asleep, but I must have. In my dreams I was flying, and Theron flew next to me, holding my hand. The dream went on and on, and for the first time in a year, I was truly happy.

I woke up smiling, and Theron was still there, sleeping next to me. I blinked.

Gruffy stood over us with a smile of his own. He clicked his beak together and nodded at me. "Squeak told me. This is your brother?"

Theron came awake, startled. He scrambled to his feet and started to grow, shoulders widening, arms thickening as he faced off with Gruffy. Little mirror plates began to cover his body. *Clack clack clack.* His hair lengthened into Darthorn's long mane.

"Be at ease, protector," Gruffy said. "I want nothing but safety for you and your sister."

Darthorn stood there, taller than Gruffy and implacable, the shield gleaming on his arm.

"But the time is upon us," Gruffy continued. "We must take to the air again."

"I'm coming with you," Darthorn said in his deep voice.

"We would be honored by your company. And I know that if there is fighting before this is done, your prowess will be most helpful."

"You're going to the sea?" Darthorn rumbled.

"Yes," Gruffy said.

"I will meet you there." He strode toward the trees. The giant pug stood waiting, and he leapt onto its back.

"Wait!" I shouted, running up to him. "You're going?"

"I'll follow you, Lore. I have since you got here."

"I'll see you at the sea, then."

He nodded.

"Well then, let's go!" I said.

We flew through morning, yellow light glinting off the colorful trees. I felt more awake than I ever had. I breathed the fresh air and put my hands out to cup the wind.

"Lady Lorelei!" Ripple gasped, clenching my waist tightly.

I yelled into the wind just for the joy of it, just to hear my own voice flying back at me.

Gruffy glanced over his shoulder, the edge of his beak curled up in a smile. He screeched at the sunrise with me.

"Put thy hands down! I beg of thee!" Ripple said.

I laughed, and Gruffy screeched again.

By midday, we reached the ocean.

Gruffy circled and landed on soft, white sands. The turquoise sea was breathtaking, except for one part a little ways out, in the very center. Thunderclouds roiled and the water was dark. I felt my heart sink as I looked at it. The black mass of clouds seemed alive as lightning burst within them, lighting their bubbling underbellies. Rain poured on the water below. That was the same storm that had taken my parents. Looking at it, I felt small and helpless like I did that night.

To the right of the thunderclouds, the burning red gash in the sky glowed, bigger than ever.

Gruffy knelt so that Ripple and I could dismount. The great griffon's eyelids half-covered his large eyes. He looked tired. I thought of the vicious roaches and how valiantly he had fought. He had been so scratched, but either he healed really fast, or his fur and feathers covered the damage from view.

"Gruffy, you've been flying forever. We should rest," I said.

"You are kind, Doolivanti. But I am fine."

Pip flapped overhead. "He'll go till he drops. Go till he drops."

"Pip exaggerates. I am fine. I shall rest my wings. A griffon recovers strength simply walking instead of flying."

"A griffon is the most stubborn creature in Veloran. The most stubborn creature in Veloran."

Gruffy's tail lashed back and forth on the white sand. Pip flapped away, hovering at a safe distance.

I turned to the forest bordering the beach. Darthorn emerged from the trees, light gleaming off the mirrored plates and thorns of his armor. The plates receded and he shrank to his normal size.

I ran toward him.

"How do you get here so quickly?" I hugged him because I could. Just because he was here and he was alive and it was the most wonderful thing ever.

"HuggyBug does it," he said.

"Who?"

He pointed at the giant pug, who stood at the edge of the forest, watching with his mirrored eyes.

"HuggyBug the pug?" I said.

Theron looked down and dug his bare foot into the sand. "I know. It's not very cool. It's just, I was scared when I got here.

That's what I called him. When I became Darthorn, I tried to call him 'Spike,' 'cause it sounded better. But he didn't answer to that name."

"HuggyBug is way better," I said. "Does he always run that fast?"

"Oh, he doesn't run," Theron replied. "He blinks. He just sort of blinks and the trees move. He can go anywhere in the forest, but he can't go past it. See?" He looked up where HuggyBug stood, right at the edge of the trees, but not beyond. "He won't come out onto the sand."

"Will he be okay?" I asked. "If you leave?"

"Ha! Nothing messes with HuggyBug. He showed me everything I know about the forest."

We returned to the group, and I looked at the stormy ocean.

"Tis my home," Ripple said softly. "My realm. And tis held hostage by shadows and darkness." She sighed. "An' thou wouldst follow me, I shall show thee the Sea as she was meant—"

"My friends," Gruffy interrupted. Everyone turned, following his gaze.

A dozen giant creatures rose out of the rolling surf, waves crashing on translucent shells. They were as tall as Gruffy, spidery legs lifting their oval bodies high into the air. Red eyes on tall stalks peered down from a great height, and they held their pincers even higher.

"Everything in Veloran is huge," I murmured. "What are they?"

"Grumpalons," Ripple said, her voice as calm as the still wind. "They were ever protectors of my realm, patrolling this shore for villains." Her dark blue eyebrows came down over her all-blue eyes.

"Caution, princess." Gruffy stepped forward and flexed his wings. "There are many. Perhaps we retreat and find another entrance to the Sea?"

"A wise plan if I ever heard one," Pip squawked. "If I ever heard one."

The princess didn't seem to be listening to either of them. Her gaze remained on the advancing Grumpalons.

"Let us—" Gruffy began.

The princess strode across the sand toward the frightening giant crabs. Her dress rippled like the tide.

"Princess!" Gruffy called after her.

"There she goes. There she goes."

With a single leap, Gruffy drew alongside the princess. The Grumpalons had almost reached them.

"Princess, we have no plan," Gruffy said. "I will happily give my life for your cause, but we cannot win this battle."

Ripple looked at Gruffy, her eyes flashing. "Grumpalons were charged with the protection of my realm." She waved her hand at the roiling storm over the murky sea. "I shall call them to task."

"Prudence, perhaps, is—"

"I shall call them to task!" She started forward again.

Gruffy was silent, then said, "Indeed, princess." He turned his noble head to face the line of advancing Grumpalons.

Now that they were so close, I realized I'd misjudged them. They weren't huge, they were enormous! They loomed over Gruffy, taller than elephants. Their translucent arms were thick and covered with bumps that, in some places, sloped to spikes and looked to be as hard as Darthorn's armor. Their pincers were as long as my arms. They spread out, surrounding us.

Theron grew. Mirrored armor flew across his body, coming together. *Clack clack clack.* In seconds, Darthorn stood defiantly on the other side of Ripple.

Pip flew high above, out of reach. Squeak perched atop Gruffy's head, his tiny marble eyes flicking from one Grumpalon to the next. I wondered if the mouse was formulating a plan. I wished I had a plan. Was there any kind of plan that would work? We were outnumbered ten to one.

"Thou darest accost us, Grumpalons?" Ripple said to the nearest. "Tis thy charge to protect these shores!"

I thought of frail Ripple in the tunnels of Azure City. I thought of frightened Ripple flying on Gruffy's back. Neither of those girls was anywhere to be found. I smiled, watching Ripple write her own story.

The Grumpalons came to a stop.

"It is our sworn duty," the lead Grumpalon said, a wide mouth splitting the front of his oval body. "To serve the ruler of the Sea."

"And when the ruler of the Sea wast bound and caged and supplanted, didst thou think nothing of swearing thy allegiance to the villain who didst supplant her?" Ripple asked.

The Grumpalon twitched as if she'd poked it with a stick.

"Didst thou curl into thy shell when the shadow settled over the Sea, Montregon?" She addressed him by name. "What assailed thy senses that thou wouldst assist this Ink King?"

A rumble went through Grumpalons, their big mouths opening, closing and making burping sounds.

"Princess Ripellia?" the lead Grumpalon said. Burps rumbled around the circle.

"It bespeaks well that thou dost recognize thy princess. What didst thou, with all thy might, whilst my realm was taken and I imprisoned?"

The Grumpalons bobbed up and down. "The fighting was finished before we reached the palace, princess. Ratsharks and Beetlins infest the sea. We could not best them."

"And tell me, Grumpalon, how fiercely didst thou strive?"

The Grumpalons shifted, pushing white sand. After a moment, they settled and the leader spoke again.

"They took the Grumplings, princess. They slew half our number and took our small ones."

Ripple's hands unclenched and she stepped forward. The sea surged toward her, sloshing around her ankles. Her dress mixed with the water, then became a swirling pillar that lifted her up above the Grumpalons. She put a hand on the towering crab's shell between its eye stalks.

"'Tis a grievous crime," she said softly. "Were I in thy position, I might have taken thy course." She turned, looking down at each of the Grumpalons in turn. "And yet, a year has passed since this villainous Ink King has come to rule. Wouldst thou wait forever for thy Grumplings?"

The lead Grumpalon shifted. "The Ratsharks are without number. They infest the sea and the palace. We could not oust them the first time. What hope have we now?"

"With thine allies," Ripple said with finality. "Together, and only thus, might we find hope." She raised her arms over her head. "I have returned, and I bring the life of the Eternal Sea with me. United, let us show this Ink King where shadows belong."

The Grumpalons started bobbing up and down.

"Wouldst thou follow thy princess into battle?" she demanded. "Given this second chance, wouldst thou uphold thy oath and take back thy small ones?"

The Grumpalons bobbed up and down vigorously.

"I have returned to bring justice to this villain and any who stand with him. An' thou dost see this as thy duty, then follow me, for I stand before thee."

The Grumpalons flicked sand and water with their mighty legs, their claws scraping deep.

Gruffy screeched his approval.

"Spread word to thy fellows! We swim upon the palace and soon! An' they would stand by our sides, we shall retake our kingdom!"

The Grumpalons burped and flicked their legs as they turned and scuttled toward the water. In moments, the white beach was empty except for a thousand Grumpalon prints in the sand. The sea withdrew down the beach, lowering Ripple back down.

"That was amazing!" I said.

Ripple turned toward me, and she sighed. "'Twas but a step, and a small one at that." Her inspiring confidence faded. "The Grumpalons did not deceive. An army stands twixt us and victory. Needs must we raise our own that we might stand even the slightest chance."

"I'm not afraid of Ratsharks," Darthorn said.

"He speaks for us all," Gruffy agreed.

"Squeak!"

"I guess we won't be home for dinner. I guess we won't be home for dinner," Pip squawked, flapping overhead.

"Jimmy's gonna give back everything," I said.

"What other allies might we count upon?" Gruffy asked.

"Such a course lies not straight. There are but two who might aid us. Ratsharks and Beetlins never lived in my kingdom ere now. They would not be inclined to assist us, I daresay. The Swisherswashers, perchance. Or the Flimflams." She paused. "Though the Flimflams may be a fool's errand."

"Why?" I asked.

"Verily, they are unpredictable. And mad as a . . ." She seemed to search for the right word, and then shrugged.

"You mean crazy."

Ripple looked at me. "Indeed, milady. I have not quite the proper speech. In thy world, when one is truly and thoroughly mad, what wouldst one be compared to?"

"Um." I thought of *Alice in Wonderland*. "Mad as a March Hare. Or mad as a Hatter."

"Well, in Veloran, if thy wits are wild," Ripple said as she began walking up the beach, "we say thou art 'mad as a Flim-flam.'"

CHAPTER *16*

WE MARCHED UP THE BEACH TOWARD A LARGE STAND OF Silverweft trees that stood apart from the Kaleidoscope Forest. The center was an enormous circle, and lines of trees meandered out into the sea, creating little bays between. It seemed as though they had been placed just so.

"I've never met a Flimflam before," Gruffy said. "Though I have heard stories."

"What are they?" I asked.

"Um." He seemed at a loss for words. "Well, they are Flimflams."

No sooner had I asked the question than I saw a creature emerge from the Silverweft tree. At first glance, it looked like a gangly green bird. It meandered unsteadily back and forth as though it hadn't quite gotten control of its wings. I squinted to try to see it better.

It dropped, rose again, then disappeared behind the silver branches.

"We have been noticed," Ripple said.

"Shall we fly up there?" Gruffy asked.

"I could go look. I could go look," Pip offered.

"Squeak."

"Noble Squeak speaks aright," Ripple said. "Let us bide a moment. Twould be best to curry an invitation first."

"Can we be certain they will remember we are down here?" Gruffy asked. "Flimflams are not known for their focus."

"Yet Flimflams are drawn to the unusual. And we are a notable group." Ripple surveyed us. "A noble griffon. An eloquent toucan. A most clever mouse, the Mirror Man of the Kaleidoscope Forest and a Doolivanti."

"And a lovely princess. A lovely princess," Squeak said.

Ripple smiled at Pip. "I hardly think a Flimflam could resist us." She turned her gaze back to the tall stand of Silverweft trees.

Sure enough, six Flimflams flew up out of the leaves, each a different color: red, blue, black, yellow, purple, and green. Gruffy, ever protective, took a step forward.

"Nay, good griffon. I fear not the Flimflams." Ripple stepped in front of him.

As the Flimflams neared, I realized I had been wrong. They weren't weird birds. They were flying foxes.

They landed gracefully in front of Ripple, folding their wings against their backs, and each changed as they moved forward, growing thinner, taller, becoming half-human/half-fox. The metamorphosis was so smooth that I blinked.

They stood upright, about as tall as me, and were covered in colored fur. They had doglike legs, fox faces, big bushy tails, and the body and arms of a slender human. All save one. One wasn't a Flimflam at all, but a black snake with wings and a small piece of steel wrapped around its flat head just behind the eyes, like some kind of hastily made helmet.

The purple Flimflam wore thin silver gloves, and he stepped to the front of the group.

The green Flimflam scurried to stand beside the black snake and drew a brush from a pouch at his side. He began to paint the air above the sand with quick strokes. A roll of carpet appeared before the purple Flimflam.

The green Flimflam knelt and flipped the carpet toward us. It rolled out, covering the sand and ending an inch away from Ripple's webbed toes.

"*Gracias,* Sir Vant," said the purple Flimflam. He looked up at the princess and cocked his head. "You are the sea princess." He stepped onto the carpet with his dog paws, his wings flexing. He had silver eyes. "And you are . . . so beautiful. Walking poetry. A painting in motion. A cool flame that lights the water." He had a light Latino accent, like a couple of the kids at my school who were from Mexico. Except his accent was a little bit different. He raised a silver hand and waved it as though he was conducting an orchestra.

"They gird themselves for war," the blue Flimflam—who stood

behind the leader—said in a toneless voice. "The princess emerges from the forest and puts the Grumpalons in a state of rebellion. She wants her kingdom back from the Ink King."

"Ah, *bueno,* Sir Ebral. I believe you are right," the purple Flimflam said.

"I'm always right," Sir Ebral replied drily.

The purple Flimflam raised an eyebrow, though he kept his gaze on Ripple.

"Ninety-eight percent of the time," Sir Ebral amended.

The purple Flimflam adjusted the angle of his hand, and I realized he wasn't conducting unheard music. He was painting Ripple with an invisible brush. A chill ran up my spine and I thought about how I had come to Veloran. I had written my own story—the story I wanted—on the air with an invisible pencil. And I had changed my life.

The green Flimflam had painted the carpet and made it real. I wondered if the purple Flimflam was doing something to Ripple she couldn't see. I stepped forward to stop him.

The purple Flimflam turned his gaze to me.

His hand hovered in front of Ripple's face, unmoving. He stood there for a long, quiet moment, then spoke again.

"You . . ." He glanced at the fiery gash in the sky, then back at me. "I dreamed of you. I dreamed you were coming. The girl with the midnight hair and eyes of the evening sky." He peeled his silver gloves off and let them go. They wobbled, turning into spheres of water and floated right next to him. He moved toward me, and as he did, he transformed further, becoming human: a teenage boy barely older than me. He had a straight, pointed nose, black wavy hair to his shoulders and tanned skin. His eyes were the same glinting silver color they had been when he was a fox. He wore loose purple pants and a purple vest over his bare chest. "You are from Earth . . ." he murmured, then reached out to touch my face.

Gruffy rumbled in his chest, but Ripple put a hand on the griffon's feathery mane. "Bide," she murmured.

I caught the purple Flimflam boy's hand, keeping him from touching my face, and turned his gesture into an awkward handshake.

"Pleased to meet you." His fingers were slender and strong.

The purple Flimflam smiled, revealing shining white canine teeth. "You are not supposed to be here." He echoed what Jimmy had said.

"I . . ." I began.

The green Flimflam scurried over to the purple Flimflam, keeping low to the ground. He tugged on the leader's pant leg.

The purple Flimflam looked down as though just noticing he wasn't alone with me. "*Sí*, of course, Sir Vant." He stepped back and my panic subsided. The way he looked at me, into me . . . It was as if he knew my entire history at a glance.

"*Por favor*, allow me to make introductions," the purple Flimflam said. "I am Sir Real, first painter of the Flimflams." He gestured to the green Flimflam who was so bent over that his head barely came up to Sir Real's waist. "This is Sir Vant."

He turned, gesturing to the blue Flimflam. "Behind me is Sir Ebral."

"In point of clarification," Sir Ebral said in his monotone, "we are not all painters."

"And beside Sir Ebral," Sir Real continued, pointing at the yellow Flimflam, "is Sir Kewitous."

"Thank you," Sir Kewitous said. "I'd been on my platform all day, not that the day is very old. That is to say, I'd been wanting an excuse to take a break from the cookies I'd been painting. I do love them, and was trying to get them just right before I ate them, you see. At any rate, at that moment my brother, Sir Cuhl, rolled in. He wasn't the one to tell me that you were approaching, though. I daresay he wasn't aware himself. But he had smelled the cookies, you see, and he loves cookies. And he did precede Sir Vant, who had been sent to gather us at the behest of Sir Real. Which, after a brief flight, led me here. And so I owe you for giving me my needed break. My point is: it is a pleasure to meet you."

Sir Real smiled, as though he had anticipated a lengthy speech from Sir Kewitous, and moved on to the red Flimflam, who stood straight, one finger in the air as though he was about to say something.

"This is Sir Tain," Sir Real said.

"Absolutely!" Sir Tain bellowed, slicing his finger down emphatically.

"And last . . ." Sir Real gestured at the black winged snake and paused. "This is Sir Pent."

Sir Pent flapped up and nodded his head vigorously. His makeshift helmet flew off his head and clanged on the ground. He hissed, dove down to recover it, and came back up with it askew on his head again.

"And we are all most happy to meet you," Sir Real finished.

"Squeak," said Squeak.

"I'm not particularly happy," Sir Ebral said.

"But do not let that upset you," Sir Real interjected smoothly. "He is never happy."

"It is important to note," Sir Ebral said, "that none of us should be happy. Too many possibilities remain uncalculated to know if we'll even live out the day."

Sir Real smiled affectionately, then turned to me. "Sir Ebral sees himself as a realist. That is funny, no?"

Sir Ebral frowned.

"Well, this is Gruffy the griffon," I said. Gruffy nodded, his head high above the Flimflams. "And Pip the toucan."

"Pleased to meet you. Pleased to meet you." Pip flapped overhead.

"Squeak the mouse," I said.

"Squeak." Squeak smoothed his whiskers and bowed.

"And this is the Mirror Man. He's also my brother Theron. And Princess Ripple of the Eternal Sea," I finished, indicating Ripple.

Sir Real smiled slyly. "A blind Flimflam I would be," Sir Real said, "if I could not recognize the sea princess. But you, what is your name?"

"I am Lorelei."

Sir Real raised an eyebrow. "This is your name?"

"Yes."

"All of your name?" He glanced at Ripple then back at me. "*Cierto?*"

"Yes."

"Told you. Told you," Pip squawked.

"Hmm." Sir Real raised his hand and gave a careful flip to his wrist as though he was painting a curve on my face. This captured his attention for a moment. I worried again that he was casting some kind of spell, but I didn't feel anything and nothing happened.

"We need your help," I said.

Sir Real lowered his hand, then raised it again and brushed some light strokes. "The air holds its breath around you." He nodded respectfully. "Doolivanti."

"Ripple needs your help," I stammered. "The Ink King has taken her kingdom. And . . ." I paused. "And, my brother and I," I nodded at Theron, who was like a statue in his brilliant mirrored armor, "we need your help. The Ink King has taken our parents, too."

Sir Real looked up at the tall Mirror Man. "You seek revenge," Sir Real murmured as he tried to see past Theron's mirrors. "The taste it leaves, they say, is cold."

"I don't want revenge," I said.

"No?" Sir Real asked, his gaze lingering on Theron a moment longer, then turning back to me.

"We cannot help them," Sir Ebral interjected. "The odds of wresting the sea kingdom from the Ratsharks and the Beetlins are ten to one."

"And overcoming the Ink King who rules there, impossible." Sir Real paused. "But not for her, I think." He dabbed at the air on my left side, then considered me as though trying to decide if I needed more color.

"The Ink King is a thief," Sir Real said. "Of kingdoms and

mothers and others, you say. But you brought yourself here without invite to stay. You opened a gate and pushed yourself through. The Ink King is mild next to the danger of *you*."

All of my companions turned to look at me.

"What? I'm not a threat!" I said. "I came here looking for my family. A family that Jimmy stole!"

"I am sure that this is true," said Sir Real. "Which is why we should know more of you."

"If you think I . . ." I paused. "What?"

"Of course!" exclaimed Sir Tain.

"That is not the obvious conclusion," Sir Ebral refuted, flustered.

"No, it is not," Sir Real said. "Not one jot."

Sir Ebral said, "Good sense demands that—"

"She is a threat," Sir Real continued. "That I get. But she is also Destiny's pet."

"Stop rhyming," Sir Ebral said.

"*Claro,* what will Destiny do if we cast her aside, do you think?" Sir Real asked.

Sir Ebral thought about this for a moment, putting his furry blue fingers to his chin.

"What do you mean?" I asked.

"There is more to you than I yet know. Would it be wise to let you go?"

"Rhyming is an inefficient way to speak." Sir Ebral frowned. "For the safety of your trees, tell her to leave."

"Send her away and she'll come back. Her army marches to attack," Sir Real said.

Sir Ebral sighed. "You never listen to good sense."

"Good sense is as good sense does. As hard as nails or soft as fuzz. Sense is in all things we know. Good or bad, fast or slow. Flip side up or right side down. Take heart, good Sir, and lose your frown. I cannot cast this glint aside. That, my wonder can't abide. We'll rely upon my hunch. We'll take them in and feed them lunch. What hurt to look and then take stock? Fate's pet and I shall have a talk."

"Absolutely!" Sir Tain exclaimed.

Sir Pent hissed, wriggling in excitement. Sir Ebral rolled his eyes.

"I invite you to my humble home," Sir Real said, bowing low to me. "Which is better with friends than it is alone."

CHAPTER *17*

THE FLIMFLAMS CHANGED INTO THEIR WINGED FOX FORMS
and took to the air. Theron shrank to his normal size, and he,
Ripple, and I climbed aboard Gruffy. He leapt into the air with
a powerful flapping and took us all up toward the giant Silverweft trees.

I had seen a few Silverwefts as we had flown over the forest,
but none even half this size. The graceful silver limbs wove upward and together, lacing back and forth, creating a braid of
branches with spaces through which the Flimflams darted and

disappeared. Gruffy followed them and landed on a floor of silver branches woven together like a basket. The walls were made the same way. Everything grew straight from the tree. There were no hard corners or places where boards had been nailed together.

I jumped off Gruffy, and the woven floor bounced me up like a trampoline. "Bouncing braided branches!" I giggled, looking at Theron.

No sooner had we arrived than the green Flimflam arrived, deftly painting a table into existence and setting an empty tray down on it. Then he began painting on the tray. Luscious-looking grapes appeared under the deft purple strokes of his brush, then sandwiches as he brushed their right angles, the crusts of the bread.

He nodded at me. I took one of his magical sandwiches and bit into it. Chicken salad!

I went to the edge of the balcony, which had no rails, as I munched on the delicious snack and finished it. The drop was dizzying, the gentle surf lapping the white sands far below, millions of silver leaves in between. I guess creatures who could fly didn't need rails.

Veloran's white-streaked sky seemed closer than the blue sky of Earth. The Eternal Sea by the shore was turquoise, deepening to dark blue farther out, and then black as it joined with the storm. Behind me, the Kaleidoscope Forest began with its speckled mix of purples, greens, blues, yellows, reds, and browns. Everything here was brighter and richer than on Earth.

"It is stunning, no?" Sir Real came up beside me in his boy form.

I looked at him. It was unsettling how he kept shifting from form to form. "Did it take lots of practice? Turning from a fox to a human?"

He smirked.

"What?" I said.

"*Perdóneme.* I apologize. I laugh at your expense." He bowed. "I am human."

"You're a Doolivanti? From Earth?"

"I am."

"How many of us are there?"

"Some."

"Why is everyone here allergic to giving straight answers?"

He grinned. "Not all Doolivantis are from Earth."

"You mean, there are people from other planets?"

"Other planets. Other . . . places."

"Where—"

"But none that I have ever seen like you, *chica*." He interrupted me. "Those who transform, yes. Those who make themselves into what they want to be. Like your brother. Like me. But none like you."

"What do you mean?"

He gestured with his hands; he didn't have the silver gloves this time, and I wondered where they went when he wasn't wearing them or making them hover in the air as silver bubbles. "There is a heat all around you." He paused. "And a danger. I am not sure Veloran has seen anything like you, either."

"I'm not dangerous, like you think."

"Oh, but you are."

"I don't want to hurt anyone!"

He paused, watching me. "I believe you. But you will. *Claro.*" He pointed to his left. The burning gash took up an entire corner of the sky, and it was bigger than before. "You did that, did you not?"

"I don't know." My heart hurt. I thought of the tiny burning thread that had come out of my chest when I first followed Gruffy.

Sir Real looked at me skeptically. "I think that you do. That appeared in the sky two days ago. How long have you been here?"

I looked away.

He jostled me with his elbow, and his serious tone changed. "*Chica,* I am not judging. Much." He smirked. "Veloran calls to children. And you have better reason to be here than most. But . . ."

I looked back at him. "But what?"

"You forced your way in, no? You did something different."

"I had to find my family!"

"Did Veloran offer you something? A new face? New clothes? A new name?"

Loremaster . . .

I felt my face flush. I thought of the beautiful blue-and-silver jacket, the leggings, and the silver boots. I thought of the burn in my chest when I had denied the persona that had been offered to me.

I waited until my voice was steady. "What about you? Why are you here?"

"Ah," he said ruefully. "I am a painter. Since I was old enough to hold a brush."

"You're here 'cause you paint?"

"My father sent me to prep school, 'with a strong math and science focus.'" He affected a deeper voice. "'Something worthwhile. None of this slapping paint on canvas nonsense.'" He paused, drew a breath. "So I showed him. I ran away, and Veloran, she found me."

"Found you?"

"I was thirteen."

"How long have you been here?"

He didn't answer me, but grinned instead. He was very fox-like when he did that.

"And how did Veloran find you?" He turned my question on me instead.

I shrugged. "I just . . . Gruffy showed up in my house. He said I pulled him into my world, and asked me to—"

Sir Real held up a hand. "A moment, *por favor*. You pulled a griffon to Earth?"

"I-I don't know."

"You keep using those words. For someone who does not know much, you certainly *do* a lot."

"For someone who's mostly a fox, you certainly talk a lot," I retorted. "I didn't do it on purpose!"

"So you accidentally did the impossible. That makes me feel much better about you." He paused with a wry smile, and when I didn't say anything, he said, "I have never heard of anyone who could take part of Veloran back to Earth. Not even a twig, much less a whole griffon."

"Well . . ."

"What do you know about Veloran?" Sir Real asked.

"I know that I've seen more in only a few days here than a full year back home," I said. "I heard it's called the Wishing World."

"*Zam*. Yes. Who told you that?"

I pressed my lips into a firm line. I didn't want to talk about Jimmy. Sir Real didn't push it.

"Okay, let me tell you what I know," he said. "In Veloran, children get what they want. You arrive here, Veloran paints you in clothes that fit you, with your true name, and you find things you like right away. For me, the Flimflams found me. They are fun. They fill the world with color and art and silliness. They teach me what I want to know, just by being here. I found them because I was meant to find them." He shrugged. "This does not happen by accident in Veloran. It is not like home. I think maybe that I made the Flimflams. You know? That I wanted them, or something like them, and Veloran made them for me." He glanced over to where Gruffy lay, preening his wing. Every now and then, the griffon's huge eye would swivel to glance at us, then focus back on his work. "I think you are the same."

"What do you mean?"

"Your creations over there."

"I didn't make Gruffy. Or Pip and Squeak. They were here when I got here."

"This is what I mean," he said. "It is not like I waved my brush and the Flimflams appeared. They found me, surrounded me. Cared for me. What did you most need when you came here?" He gave a sly glance at Gruffy. "A protector? It makes me wonder what the toucan is for you. He is caring but silly. He repeats everything he says. On Earth, this is what adults are for you, maybe? And this mouse, they give respect to him like he knows what they do not. They listen to what he says, though he squeaks only. He is the wise one in your group. Do you sometimes feel that you cannot hear your own wisdom? Do you sometimes not *want* to hear it? They are very curious companions."

I blinked, unable to look away from Gruffy. He was magnificent. He was . . . perfect.

"You came looking for family, yes?" Sir Real asked.

"*My* family."

"Well, that is what they are." Sir Real looked at Gruffy, Pip, and Squeak.

Gruffy kept his protective gaze on me as he settled his head on top of his mighty talons. I turned away. Sir Real watched me with one of his dark eyebrows raised, waiting for my response.

"What was your name, on Earth?" I asked.

He seemed surprised, and opened his mouth to say something, but stopped himself. "I do not go by this name anymore. No one in Veloran uses their name from before."

"Well, I'm not from Veloran, and I'm not calling you 'Surreal.'"

He chuckled. "No?"

"No."

"And here is a question for you, Lorelei: why do you *not* have a new name? Every Doolivanti does."

"That's not . . ." I began, and stopped. Theron . . . Darthorn and the Mirror Man. Jimmy, the Ink King. Sand Spinner and Sky Captain and the Leaf Laugher.

Loremaster . . .

"I didn't . . . My name is Lorelei."

He paused, raising one of his black eyebrows. "I think this is part of how you are different. I have never seen anyone cause a rip like this." He pointed at the red fire in the sky. "Veloran did not shape you as it shapes us. Look at me, at your brother. We have been altered. But not you. You march across Veloran on a mission, wearing your own skin and using your own name."

"Well . . ." I started to say.

"Veloran showed me what I wanted to be. But you already knew, I think."

A bell rang in the back of my mind. *I will write my own story.*

"I just wanted my family back," I said. "I didn't want to hurt anyone else."

"How did you do it?" he asked. "How did you come here?"

"What is your real name?" I shot back.

He smiled a tight smile. "I do not want to tell you."

"Why not?"

He looked away, out over the dark sea. "Because I do not want to go back," he whispered. "I do not want to be ordinary again. If I say my name, I will hear my father speaking, and then I will have to go home."

Suddenly, he was just a boy, not some mystical creature who could shift back and forth between a fox and a human. He was just a boy afraid of his father.

"Nobody is ordinary," I said softly.

He let out a breath, and didn't speak for a long time. "I do not know whether I like you or I hate you." He looked back at me. "I have never met anyone who made me feel safe and scared at the same time."

"I don't mean to make you scared."

He let out a breath.

"You know," he finally said. "I have watched the colors of the sea darken on my palette this past year. I saw the storm start. Mostly I do not pay attention to what is going on outside these trees, but it is hard to ignore when the sea turns cold. The storm has been out there a long time, getting larger. I knew that something was coming. But I did not expect you."

"Jimmy is the one who is making the sea dark, not me."

"Ah. Jimmy is from Earth. This is the Ink King?"

"Yes."

"And he took your parents."

"And Ripple's kingdom."

"He is not good for Veloran."

"I know."

"But you are worse." He glanced at the burn in the sky. "The Ink King took his kingdom by force. But he did not rip the world."

I swallowed and tried not to show how much those words hurt.

"Well, the sooner I get my parents, the sooner . . ." I cleared my throat, but the lump didn't go away. "The sooner I can leave."

He nodded, and for a long moment, he just watched the gash of fire. Then he clapped his hands, and the loud noise startled me. "Then let us begin. Your princess will need more soldiers. Shall we?" He extended his hand, and as he did, purple fur grew on it. Wings rose up from his back. His nose lengthened until his face became a fox's face.

"Right now?" I asked.

"There is only one hand on a Veloran clock," Sir Real said. "And it always points to 'now.'"

CHAPTER *I8*

Sir Real spoke a few quiet words to Sir Vant, and the green Flimflam flew up through the leaves, high into the sky, and painted bright pink letters across the dark horizon: Flimflams to the beach!

The entire tree shook as multicolored Flimflams shot from between its branches, each one gliding down to the gentle surf and landing in clusters among the waiting giant Grumpalons. There were hundreds of Flimflams, each different from the next.

One had red and orange fur swirled together. One had blue and green. There was a zebra-striped Flimflam, a giraffe-spotted Flimflam. I marveled at them, all of them, wondering if they had come from Sir Real's palette. Had they all sprung up from his imagination? Or had some been here already? Had Huggy-Bug sprung from Theron's imagination?

Gruffy came to me and I climbed on his back, as did Ripple and Theron. He leapt from the tree and dropped like a stone over the combined armies of Grumpalons and Flimflams. Ripple yelped.

Gruffy flared at the last second, opening his wings and swooping over the sand, then rose suddenly and landed. The force of his stop pressed Theron into Ripple, Ripple into me, and me into his feathery neck. Gruffy screeched with excitement.

"Yeah!" Theron jumped from Gruffy's back and thumped onto the sand. "Flying rules!"

"Ooooh," Ripple moaned, clinging to my waist. "I like not the idea of war, but I shall be joyous to clash with the Ink King if only the fight may happen 'neath the waves, and not in the air."

Ripple waded happily up to her knees in the water. Her sparkling dress blended with the sea and turned the same turquoise color. Hundreds of Grumpalons marched farther out to sea, but still towered over the surface, shifting back and forth at the sight of their princess.

She nodded to them, holding up her hands. They calmed.

Ripple turned back to us. "I do fear, my most stalwart friends, that needs must we part company now. My path lies beneath the surface in parley with the Swisherswashers. With them, we shall have a force that may yet break the iron hold of the Ink King and his Ratsharks."

"No, good princess," Gruffy said. "We will stay with you."

She smiled gently. "Truly, I could not have asked for more valiant companions. I would take thee with me an' I might. But, prithee tell me, how wouldst thou breathe water as I do?"

Gruffy glanced up toward Squeak, who rode upon his head. I wondered if he could see the mouse.

"Squeak."

Gruffy looked back at the princess. "We shall travel up for air as needed."

"Dost know what the Ratsharks call those who bob on the surface?" Ripple asked.

Gruffy shook his head.

"Food," she said.

"Let them try." Gruffy's neck feathers rose.

"Squeak."

"What is he is saying?" I whispered to Sir Real.

Sir Real grinned. "I cannot understand a word. But I am sure it is very wise." He winked at me.

I looked at him. "You're making fun of me?"

"*Nunca*," he said through his grin. "Never."

I frowned. I felt like I was missing the best parts of the conversation when Squeak talked.

"Squeak squeak," Squeak persisted.

"He has a point. He has a point," Pip squawked.

"The Ink King seeks only an opportunity such as this," Gruffy said. "I do not like letting you go without us. He will strike immediately if we do."

"Squeak."

"Indeed." Gruffy nodded. "And he is Doolivanti. Would you pit yourself against him, knowing you had no Doolivanti to aid you?"

"Needs must I do just this," Ripple said. "I shall send thee word ere I have broken through the Ratsharks. An' thou might meet me on mine island?"

"Your island?" I asked.

Ripple pointed at the impenetrable storm far out at sea. "Mine palace lies atop a beautiful island. Thou canst not see it in the foul darkness, but thou shalt, ere we are done. We shall lift the shadows and make it again what it once was."

I squinted at the unending rain falling on the sea. I couldn't see any island at all, but the area covered in darkness was certainly large enough to hold one.

"Fare thee well, my friends," Ripple said. "I shall send thee a sign, an' thou might meet me at the palace." She hugged each of them in turn, then started into the ocean. The Flimflams changed one by one, feathered wings becoming fins and flippers. Furry feet became webbed.

"You can do that?" I turned to Sir Real.

"Are they not simply so . . . surreal?" Sir Real said proudly, smiling.

Gruffy paced back and forth as Ripple started into the ocean. "This is foul," he grumbled. "That villain will concoct something if we are not there to brace him. I do not trust him."

"I don't want to be left behind, either," I agreed. What if the Ink King defeated Ripple and it made him stronger? What if Ripple defeated the Ink King and then I never found out where Jimmy was keeping my parents?

"Squeak."

I looked after Ripple, who was submerged to the waist. The entire sea seemed like the vast billowing of her dress.

"Wait!" I called.

Ripple turned.

"Maybe I can do something," I said.

"Prithee, what canst thou do?"

I raised my hand and wrote the words on the air.

Wings like fins. Feet like paddles. Hands like scoops. Water like air.

I wrote each word carefully, and they burned on the air for all to see.

Hot coals flared in my chest, and I clenched my teeth.

The ground rumbled, and the sand shifted. The whole beach shook and began sliding toward the sea. Gruffy stepped back, looking sternly at the misbehaving ground.

"What are you doing?" Sir Real said.

"Rewriting my story," I said, digging my fingers into my shoulder at the pain in my chest.

Then it did. Everything stopped. The burn. The moving sand. It all settled, and everyone was absolutely silent.

Ripple stood in the water, her mouth open.

"She is Doolivanti," Gruffy stated proudly.

"I've never seen anyone do that," Sir Real whispered.

"You can change into whatever form you want," I countered. "I just made it so we can breathe water."

"Lorelei . . ." Sir Real pointed at the sky, and I followed his gaze. The rip was enormous now. Crimson, lavender, and orange boiled out like the sky was peeling back. It stretched from the northern horizon to the edge of the Ink King's storm. Worry filled Sir Real's silver eyes.

"I . . ." I started, but I didn't know what to say.

"Come, Doolivanti." Gruffy strode into ocean until the water was up to his belly. He submerged his head and, after a moment, brought it back up, flinging sea water. "Your spell works, and the villain is waiting."

"Lorelei, wait." Sir Real put a hand on my arm.

I looked at him, felt his tension in my own body. He was right. I *was* dangerous. I was hurting Veloran.

"What would you have me do?" I asked. "Leave my parents? Never see them again? I can't do that! I'm not like you."

He drew back as though I had slapped him.

I ran and dove into the curling surf as quickly as I could. Quick enough to hide my tears.

CHAPTER *19*

I PLUNGED INTO THE WATER AND BREATHED IT IN. IT FILLED
my lungs like cool, heavy air. I coughed, my body panicking,
and for a moment I felt like I was drowning.

Then I breathed, easily and steadily. I looked around and saw
far into the water. Colorful fish flicked away from me. The white
sands looked silver, stretching forward into the blue water.

I did this, I thought. *I made myself breathe water and swim like
a fish!*

Gruffy plunged in next to me, his huge eyes looking at me as he opened his beak and fearlessly did what I had just panicked about. He smiled and nodded, then flexed his wings and shot forward like a dolphin. His triumphant screech vibrated through the water.

I swam after him, faster than I had ever done in a pool. This was completely different; this felt like my natural self, like I had been born to swim. My hands looked the same, but they cupped the water as though there were invisible webs between my fingers. My feet kicked—tennis shoes and all—like they were flippers. Pip drew alongside me, his wings flapping against the water like fins.

"This is the weirdest thing ever. The weirdest thing ever," he warbled through the water.

"I can't even believe it!" Theron said, swimming up next to me. "Lor, you're like a wizard!"

"She is Doolivanti," Gruffy said as he swam up next to us. His talons and lion's paws swept strongly through the water, keeping him upright. They all swam like fish, but none of them looked any different.

Ripple twirled through the water, and stopped just short of me, her dress flaring. The sparkles became glints reflecting the sunlight above. We might have been turned into human fish, but Ripple *was* the water. "'Tis amazing, Lady Lorelei. Thourt truly a marvel."

"And now let us find the villain. Let us oust him," Gruffy said.

"Verily." Ripple shot forward, spinning like a drill.

The Grumpalons moved quickly, their long legs working against the ocean floor, and the Flimflams swam before them.

Word of my earth-shaking magic traveled ahead of us, and

the Swisherswashers were excited to receive us. They emerged from holes in their coral palace, which looked like a pink sponge the size of a football stadium.

The Swisherswashers were giant eels. They were powerful, long and graceful, slipping through the water like kite ribbons. Each one was longer than three Gruffys put end to end. Their eyes were large and when they blinked, it seemed to take forever. They were every shade of green imaginable, from light lime to deep forest green. Some were even so dark they looked black at a distance. Only one was a different color. Their leader, Queen Swish, was the color of sunlight.

The Swisherswashers rallied immediately to Ripple's cause. Swisherswashers and Ratsharks were natural enemies, and the Swisherswashers wanted the fierce usurpers out of their sea.

I had never seen a Ratshark, but according to Pip they were a lot like Swisherswashers, except with giant rat claws and toothy heads.

The Swisherswashers brought Ripple and the rest of us into their palace and sat us in a large, circular room. They brought food, laying it on coral tables that seemed to have grown up from the ground. The sensation of chewing food with a mouthful of water was completely weird, and I concentrated on keeping my mouth shut. Everything was salty.

As Ripple and Queen Swish discussed the plan, I caught Sir Real's glance from across the room. He didn't look happy. Only Sir Real was dwelling on what I had done. The others, though surprised by the earthquake and the red light in the sky, seemed to take what I had done in stride. They did not see a danger. Or if they did, they did not connect it to me.

I could imagine what Sir Real was saying in his mind: *You should leave, Lorelei. You should go immediately, before you wreck it for the rest of us!*

I looked at the Swisherswashers clustered around Ripple, each wanting a word from their lost princess, a touch or a nod of approval. The princess responded to the attention with grace. She listened to their suggestions and her eyes sparkled. Every Swisherswasher to whom she spoke swam away with a smile and vigor in the flip of their fins.

Plans were made. Rows upon rows of Swisherswashers formed up outside the window, and rows upon rows of Grumpalons as well, what seemed like a never-ending army.

Within the hour, the army started out for the darkened center of the sea.

We had barely swum for a minute before we saw the first Ratsharks. The beasts were hideous. They were long like the Swisherswashers, but their shark skin was mottled gray and rough. They had skinny, hairy rat arms, narrow rat chests, and rat heads that seemed diseased, sprouting mismatched fangs. Their beady eyes were completely black, and their whiskers trailed from their snouts like streams of snot.

The Ratsharks gathered in a huge line before them, snapping and growling, blocking their progress toward the center of the Ink King's storm. I still could not see the island through the murk.

Jimmy floated out of the shadows. Above and behind his head was a dark octopus, pumping ink around him. It seemed to be what was enabling him to swim, and I wondered if he had cast the same sort of spell over himself as I had, letting him breathe underwater.

Jimmy pointed at us. "Get out of my kingdom. You don't belong here."

"'Tis thee who binds this land and darkens these waters. Thou dost not belong," Ripple responded, twirling forward and stopping at the head of her army. "'Tis my realm and thou wilt relinquish it."

"You're nothing!" Jimmy shouted. "The Sea is mine. I took it from you and I'm not giving it back." Jimmy's gaze fell on me. "You," he said, his voice dropping to that inhumanly low rumble. "You're the only one who matters. But you won't be staying long."

I swam forward, and Gruffy launched ahead of me, staying right between me and Jimmy. Squeak perched in his usual place, his little head bowed against the water. Pip flapped behind them. Last came Darthorn, his mirrored armor reflecting the armies all around.

"Is that your dad's plan?" I shouted. "For you to take over the Wishing World?"

Jimmy gave a skull's grin. "Oh, he'd like that. But the Wishing World is mine."

"He sent you here! I talked to him—"

"Shut up! I don't care about him and I don't care about you! Last chance, Loreliar. Get out or you'll be sorry!"

"I'm not leaving without my parents."

"We'll see," he said. "You stupid girl." Then he shouted: "Robsombulous!"

Ripple's mouth opened, stunned. The Swisherswashers swished back and forth, agitated. The Grumpalons flicked at the sand with spastic feet, looking like they had lost all control of their bodies.

Even Gruffy was stunned into silence.

"What? What does that mean?" I asked.

"He summoned the Robsombulous," Gruffy said.

"Robsombulous. Robsombulous," Pip murmured.

"What does it mean?" I asked again, exasperated.

"The Robsombulous," Gruffy whispered, "was created at the beginning of the world. Some say it is the reason Veloran exists."

"Danger. Danger," Pip squawked, flapping about.

"Why is everyone so scared? We were about to go into battle! What is scarier than that?" I asked.

"This is worse. This is worse. Appeasing the Robsombulous is unpredictable. Unpredictable."

"Choose your Wordwimble," Jimmy said.

"Choose a what?" I looked at Gruffy.

"A Wordwimble," Sir Real said, swimming up to her. "The one who will choose the first players."

"What is going on?" I asked him. "Can you give me a straight answer?"

"The Wordwimble will choose opposite members of each army, one at a time, to spell the words," Gruffy said.

"Spell? This is a stupid spelling bee?"

Gruffy looked at me sidelong. "What is a bee?"

I sighed. "Remember? I . . . never mind. They're going to fight each other by spelling words? Who cares?"

"Vanishing entirely is enough to make one care," Sir Real interjected.

"What?"

"You spell a word incorrectly, *chica*," Sir Real said, "and you are gone."

"Sucked away. Sucked away," Pip agreed.

"To where?"

"No one knows. No one knows. Far enough that no one ever comes back. Ever comes back."

A chill went up my spine. "I'm going to have to spell?" I asked. "And if I lose, I'm—"

"*Desapareces*," Sir Real said. "You vanish."

I couldn't tell if he liked the idea or not. He had avoided me since the beach.

"A Wordwimble, or you forfeit!" Jimmy yelled, his low voice rumbling through the water.

"I will be your Wordwimble," Sir Real said, swimming forward.

I opened my mouth to stop him, but didn't say anything. I didn't trust Sir Real. He wanted Jimmy gone, but I think he wanted me gone more.

Sir Real stopped in front of Jimmy. They began talking in tones that did not carry to me.

"'Tis a clever ploy," Ripple said to me. "The Robsombulous. But it shall avail them naught. They have the disadvantage. The Flimflams are quite clever."

"And we have Squeak," Gruffy said. "He has never misspelled a word in his life."

I gave Gruffy a sidelong look. Squeak had never *spoken* a word in his life, so far as I could tell.

"Why even play at all?" I asked, knowing why Jimmy had chosen this. No Flimflam or mouse was going to have the opportunity to spell anything, because Jimmy would make sure I was the first. "Why don't we just attack?"

Gruffy laughed lightly, bubbles coming out of his mouth. "That is funny, Doolivanti."

"I wasn't trying to be funny." I frowned.

Gruffy looked at me in shock. "Defy the Robsombulous?"

"Well, just not even play."

Gruffy shook his head. "No, Doolivanti. It is too late for that."

"Squeak."

"The Robsombulous abhors conflict," Ripple said. "An' thou dost fight in its presence, thou art forfeit."

"Forfeit?"

"You get sucked away. You get sucked away," Pip clarified.

"Is it that powerful?" I asked.

"So powerful," Gruffy said, "that if someone says a particularly good word, a creature will appear."

"A new animal is born from a word?" I asked.

"Indeed. Is this not how new creatures appear in your world?" Gruffy asked.

"No."

"How do new creatures appear on your world?"

"They don't."

"You don't come up with something so clever that they are born?" Gruffy asked.

"I can't wish a hippopotamus into life. I mean, people have ideas, but just because they have them doesn't make them real."

"Then what makes them real?" Gruffy asked.

"Nothing makes them real," I said. "Some things are real and some aren't. It doesn't change just because someone makes up a word. Our world isn't like that."

"Squeak."

Gruffy laughed. "Squeak says every world is like that."

I opened my mouth to tell them they were wrong, at least about Earth, but then I thought about the new gadgets people kept coming up with. New apps every day. New phones every few months. More and more. People dreaming things into existence. Like the Internet. Or the smart phone. They saw something, spoke something, had a vision, and then many others worked hard to make it happen. It wasn't as immediate as a new creature "popping" into reality. But aside from speed, what was the difference?

"Of course," Gruffy said. "To the point: Squeak says the people with which you live may simply not realize they are doing it."

"It's beginning. It's beginning," Pip squawked.

I looked back at Sir Real and Jimmy, who were nodding. Sir Real pulled out what looked like a thin, purple pancake with white eyes. It was flopping back and forth in his hand. He tossed it up and let it float down, thrashing, to the ocean floor.

"Is that the Robsombulous?" I asked.

"That is a flipperdip," Gruffy said. "To decide which Word-wimble goes first."

"Where is the Robsombulous? How do we even know it's here?" I asked.

"Can't you feel it? Can't you feel it?" Pip asked.

"Squeak."

"It is here, right now," Gruffy said. "Everywhere around."

I looked at the water, but didn't see anything besides the agitated Ratsharks, Swisherswashers, and Grumpalons. Then I began to feel the difference in the water. There was a weight that had not been there before, as though a glass dome had been pressed down over both of the armies, making the water tighter.

"I do feel it," I whispered.

"Then clear your mind, relax," Gruffy said. "And if you are called upon, spell the word correctly."

"The Ink King and I are agreed!" Sir Real shouted, looking up from the flopping purple pancake on the ocean floor. Jimmy looked upset. "The Ink King has lost the flipperdip, and so I shall begin."

Sir Real waved his invisible brush at the nearest Ratshark, who flinched.

"You," said Sir Real. "Spell 'Individulation'!"

The Ratshark's eyes bulged. It looked to the left, then to the right. The other Ratsharks slithered back, wary.

I leaned toward Gruffy, "That's not a real word!"

"Shh," said Gruffy.

"Uh," the Ratshark stammered. Then it bolted, its sharklike body thrashing mightily. It shot like an arrow away from the Wordwimbles. There was a great sucking sound, like the last water from a clogged sink going down the drain.

The Ratshark said, "Yii!"

And then it was gone.

My heart hammered. "Gruffy," I repeated. "That wasn't a word."

"The Wordwimbles aren't allowed to use words that have already been made. That would be cheating. If they do, then they are the ones who vanish."

"But I can't . . ." I said, and I felt an icy cold chill. "I can't spell a word I've never heard before."

"Why could you not?" Gruffy asked.

"Because I've never heard it before!"

He was about to answer, then Jimmy pointed at the huge, mirror-covered Darthorn. "You," Jimmy said, and then he grinned at me.

"No—" I started to say, but Pip flapped a wing in front of my mouth and held it there, his talons clinging to my shoulder.

"You can't protest. You can't protest," Pip trilled. "You'll get sucked away! You'll get sucked away!"

I watched in horror as the Ink King looked at Darthorn and said, "Spell framjacker!"

The inscrutable Darthorn waited a long moment, then said, "F-R-A-M-J-A-C-K-E-R."

"I thought we were fighting a war!" I said.

"There are wars and there are wars," Pip said.

Sir Real selected another Ratshark.

"Goobliette," Sir Real said.

The Ratshark bared its lopsided teeth, but this one seemed braver than that last. "G," it started. "O-O-B-L-I-E-T-T-E."

"Squeak," said Squeak, nodding with reluctant appreciation.

"Correct," Sir Real said. The disappointment showed on his face as he glanced at me.

Jimmy, who had been frowning since Darthorn spelled his word correctly, turned to me, and a smile split across his inky face. He pointed.

"No," I whispered. My heart constricted. "I don't want to play."

"You must, Doolivanti. There is no escape," Gruffy said.

"But—"

"Loreliar," Jimmy said. "Oh look, your favorite game."

I had never hated anyone as much as I hated Jimmy at that moment. "Let's see if you can mess it up as badly as you did before. Spell Copteroptopus."

I looked helplessly at Gruffy, but the griffon looked at me with absolute confidence. "You can do it, Doolivanti."

"Squeak."

My mind raced. I didn't even know where to start. *C*. It had to be a *C*. Everything that sounded like a *K* always started with a C.

"C," I said. "O-P-T . . ."

Jimmy leaned forward, hands twisting together in a tiny parody of his father.

"U," I said.

Jimmy whooped.

The sea swirled behind me, becoming a watery tornado.

"Doolivanti!" Gruffy shouted.

The vortex grew, moving toward me. The Grumpalons, Swisherswashers, and Flimflams drew back. Gruffy stepped in front of me.

"I shall battle it, Doolivanti," he said, wings flaring.

"No!" I said. "Stay back. I'll stop it."

I held my hand in front of me, like I was holding a pencil.

The Robsombulous stopped, I wrote. The words burned on the water in front of me. The ground shook. Grumpalons were thrown flat. Swisherswashers and Ratsharks fluttered like a giant had shaken the ocean.

The vortex shuddered, and the pain in my chest was a hot knife, stabbing.

Jimmy shouted at me through the swirling water. "This isn't

the Starfield, Loreliar! Maybe you can beat me, but you can't fight Veloran!"

Stop, I wrote on the air. I felt the Robsombulous pushing against me, forcing its magic on me. I clenched my teeth and pushed back. The vortex began to shake, and I could see red rips at its edges, just like the rips in the sky.

Sir Real swam back from me, his mouth open and his eyes fearful.

"Lorelei." Ripple put a hand on my shoulder. My concentration faltered. I looked back at her, and her blue eyes were somber. "Verily, I am sorry," she said.

"What—?"

Something smacked my feet out from under me, and I went down. The swirling water was all around me, and I couldn't see my friends or the smug Jimmy.

The vortex engulfed me and I screamed.

CHAPTER *20*

It tumbled me, and suddenly I couldn't breathe water anymore. Once, when I went to California to visit my grandparents, I had been swallowed by a big wave. It had picked me up and turned me over and over until I didn't know which way was up. I couldn't breathe, didn't know how to escape, and I had thrashed helplessly. I would probably have drowned, except Dad plucked me up, out of the wave.

The vortex was like that, except I knew no one would save

me. Maybe there wasn't even an "up" where I could catch my breath. Maybe the Robsombulous simply drowned you.

Then a blue hand reached in and grabbed me, yanked hard, and I was drawn out of the vortex.

The spinning water drained away, swirling over my head and then vanishing like mist. I wasn't in the ocean anymore. I stood in a meadow with golden sunflowers taller than I was. The sun was bright, and the white streaks across the sky were majestic. I turned, but all I could see were sunflower stalks and flowers the size of my head.

"Lorelei," came a soft voice. I turned toward the voice and stepped into an open meadow. Ripple was waiting for me.

I opened my mouth to speak, but before I could, she slowly transformed. She grew taller, and her ocean dress blushed until it was lavender. It was decorated with silver embroidery at the neckline and a heavy sash around the waist. Ripple's blue hair became tumbling dark locks curling over her forehead and cheeks. Her all-blue eyes turned lavender with the whites that a normal human would have. Her skin was paler than mine, but no longer blue. She was human, a teenager. Maybe even older.

"Ripple!"

She smiled. "Verily, I am she, but then also, I am not," she said.

The realization hit me. "You're a Doolivanti!" She wasn't a creation of the Wishing World, like Gruffy or the Flimflams; she was a creator like Sir Real and Theron. Like me.

The teenager-who-was-Ripple laughed, soft and husky. "Lorelei, thy mind is bright and agile. Full of questions and great imaginings. Thou art what this world was meant to achieve." She paused. "I felt thee ere thou didst arrive, in that first moment thou didst call to the threads and took them in hand. I had to come to see thee and be part of thy story. To look into thy heart and know thee."

"So you *are* a Doolivanti. Or are you something else?" She was by far the oldest kid I'd seen in Veloran.

"I didst don the name 'Ripple' when first I found myself at the shore of the Eternal Sea. As did thy brother at the skirt of the Kaleidoscope Forest. As did thy friend Sir Real 'neath the sparkling leaves of the Silverweft. Twas not a lie when I told thee Ripple's body was born of the Eternal Sea. As thy true name is Lorelei, mine is Vella. Vella Wren."

My mouth hung open. "Vella Wren . . . Veloran?"

She smiled, and a blush crept into her cheeks. "I am caretaker here, and so have I been for many years. I do foster the wondrous imaginations in this place, and these children who would dream to grow stronger."

"You made Veloran?"

She shook her head. "This creation belongs not to one child, but to all. Together, we do lean upon each other to make the impossible. What thy friend Gruffy flatteringly calls Veloran is but a conversation twixt the imaginings of each child. This world is a tapestry of wondrous delight made of children's voices, each talking to the other, each of their wills interweaving like threads. The tapestry is ever expanding, seeking out children on many worlds, finding new Doolivantis, inviting them with flecks of herself and weaving them into the fabric." She nodded at my necklace.

"The comet stones."

"Indeed."

"And you're the caretaker of Veloran. What does that mean?"

"An' this Wishing World dost breathe, I feel the wind. An' this Wishing World be cut, then do I bleed." She paused, then opened the side of her dress, revealing a long, red gash exactly where the little wound had been when I'd first met her.

I covered my mouth with my hand.

"Thou wouldst have destroyed the Robsombulous," she said. "This, I could not allow, not until thou didst fully understand thy actions. So I took thee away that we might converse, that thou might knowest the consequences of thy power."

"The Robsombulous didn't send me here?" I asked.

She shook her head. "'Twas I. There are far reaches of this land, and to some only I have traveled."

"You took me away so I wouldn't hurt the Robsombulous."

"Only this once, yes."

"And what about Jimmy?"

Vella gave a little sigh. "Alas, Jimmy," she said. "As with all children called here, he is wounded. His hurt doth run so deep it grips the heart. His wrath spills over to those around him. Yet through all this, some things he sees most clearly."

"He's horrible."

"'Twas Jimmy who kept his father from returning. That was no small thing."

"So he's a hero for doing the obvious? Mr. Schmindly is horrible, too."

"All creatures harbor creation and destruction alike," Vella said. "Hast thou never spit thy venom at another in thy pain, Lorelei? Hast not thy brother?"

"Jimmy isn't throwing a tantrum. He's killing people! It's psycho. Double psycho with magic on top."

Vella sighed. "Each piece of this world arises from a different child's heart. Each with their own need and their own lessons to learn. Witness thy friend, Sir Real."

I didn't like the way Vella took Jimmy's side. "Sir Real said the Wishing World created the Flimflams for him. He didn't steal them. Or kill someone to get them."

"They didst rise from his need," Vella said. "They didst become his family. As did thine own companions."

I remembered what Sir Real had said. I shook my head. "Gruffy, Pip, and Squeak were here before I got here. Gruffy was there in the rain, a year ago."

"Gruffy and his friends have been a curiosity of mine, tis true. They didst come to be after Jimmy's storm formed around the Eternal Sea, yet I knew not where from. Twas this Wishing World, Lorelei. Thou didst need a protector in that storm. An' with Jimmy's doorway open, the world did hear thee and respond, and thy griffon was born, e'en though thou had not been invited. Never have I seen this, in all my years as steward. And then thou didst go e'en further, thou didst pull thy griffon into thine own world. Thy imagination, thy will . . . Thou dost break rules I thought immutable. Thou opened thine own passage from Earth. I first felt thee then, the might of thee, straining against the fabric. Twas then I knew from whence this Gruffy the griffon had come, and this Pip and Squeak. Hastily did I attempt to invite thee. But thou didst refuse, and this Wishing World was unable to make thee into the Loremaster."

"That was you?" I said.

She nodded. "A scant few children have refused before, and this Wishing World did close the door to them, but thy will was indomitable. The door could not be closed. Thou wert stronger, an' thou didst come ahead regardless."

"You're saying Gruffy and the others are my replacement family, like Sir Real thinks." Gruffy my protector. Pip the parent. And Squeak the indecipherable book of wisdom. "So I made them for what I needed, and they're not real. Just like Jimmy said. They're paper cutouts. Video game characters."

"Oh, Lorelei. Thy passion makes noble Gruffy the most real creature in all of Veloran. Bright imagination crafts the real. Has he not grown beyond your original intent, changing more with each passing moment? Does he not deepen? Does he not ask more questions about his life and the world?"

I thought about the barrage of questions Gruffy had asked just before the Robsombulous. He'd not been curious at all when I first arrived, only filled with the need to protect.

"I'm so confused," I said.

Vella's eyes sparkled. "Thou didst come to this Wishing World already knowing what other children come to learn: how to dream. How to make dreams real. Children need this place to paint their own paintings and write their own stories, and perchance to return to their own worlds with certainty and strength." Her lavender gaze held me. "None may simply point their fingers and alter this scape as thou dost. None have defied the fabric of this Wishing World and stayed."

"Jimmy opened a doorway to Earth!"

"He is the Ink King, shaped by this Wishing World. His ability is linked to his inky shadows, which opened the veil to

Earth. He doth speak into the conversation as others before him. He didst bring adults here, which is unusual, but it has been done before. I'faith, he didst bring them under the power of this Wishing World, and so they sleep as though in a dream. Children such as Jimmy have been seen before."

"Oh, good. So because he's using the Wishing World the *right* way, he gets to kidnap people? He gets to take my parents and sling my brother into the Kaleidoscope Forest to fend for himself or die?!"

"Theron didst fend amazingly well."

"That is *so* not the point."

"Milady Lorelei, didst thou know I was a child like Jimmy when I did first arrive? Angered and helpless. Tis why this Wishing World does invite children. Here might Jimmy learn to see beauty, to feel strong and safe again. Given this dominion he believes he craves, soon shall he discover his true craving: respect and love."

"So how long does he get to figure it out? How many other people does he get to hurt before you stop him?" I asked.

Vella looked down, her pale toes digging into the grass. "We have had arguments between children before."

"Arguments? Jimmy is *killing* other Doolivantis! Just send him back to Earth!"

"Until the next Jimmy doth arrive? Or the next Lorelei . . . ?"

"The next . . ." Her words hit me hard, like she'd punched me in the chest, and I actually took a step back. "The next me?"

"Thou art exciting and terrifying and driven beyond any child I have ever seen. Thy will cuts through the wills of others as if they were paper. What thou dost dislike, thou dost change, no matter the consequence."

"I never wanted to hurt this place."

"Ah," Vella said softly. "But what dost thou wish e'en more?"

I felt hollow, and I couldn't speak.

"Yes." Vella looked down at her toes again, picking at the grass. "Thou wilt not leave without thy brother or thy parents. Thou art fiery and noble and unstoppable. Every moment thou doth persist, the fabric strains e'en more. Every command thou makest rips the world wider. And there are none who can stop thee."

"If Veloran rips, what happens to the children?" I asked.

"They shall return to their own worlds, but the conversation shall be over."

"What about Gruffy? Pip and Squeak? The Flimflams? What about those who were born here?"

"They do but live through the dreams of children. Without the children . . ." She opened her hands.

"They'll die," I whispered.

"Yes."

"Then *you* take my parents away from Jimmy. I won't use my powers and I'll . . . I'll just go," I said, and my voice broke. I held onto the feather Gruffy had given me. My link to him.

"I cannot force Jimmy to release thy parents," Vella said.

I looked at her. "But *I* can."

"This remains to be seen."

"What if . . . What if I could use just a little power to stop him, to get my parents back?"

"A little power to stop the Ink King?"

I turned away. "So what happens now?"

"Thou dost make thy choice."

"Why is it *my* choice?" I shouted, turning on her. "Why not Jimmy?"

"Because it is thy choice."

"And if I don't listen? If I say I don't care?"

"Then perhaps tis here, now, where this conversation between children and this Wishing World must end." Vella gave no indication whether this made her sad or mad or anything.

I clenched my fists.

Vella gazed at me steadily. "What dost thou wish to do?"

I looked through my tears at the beautiful meadow. I thought of Gruffy, Pip, and Squeak. HuggyBug. All the Grumpalons and the Flimflams.

Then I thought of my brother, lost for a whole year because of Jimmy's selfishness. I thought of my poor mom and dad, locked away who knows where in the sleep of the dead.

I set my jaw.

"Send me back to Jimmy." I didn't look Vella in the eyes.

She paused a moment, then said, "As you wish."

THE SUNFLOWER MEADOW BEGAN TO CHANGE. IT BECAME FLAT, like I was stepping back from a painting, and then thin strips peeled away, one after the other until the meadow was gone, revealing a blackness. I tumbled in, falling . . .

Then I was swirling through dark water. I kept my mouth shut and didn't try to breathe. My hands did not feel webbed.

My feet did not feel like flippers. I fought my way upward and broke the surface, gasping for breath.

Rain came down, pocking the top of the sea, and an island loomed in front of me. Ripple's palace stood dark against the gray rain, seven spires pointing skyward. A wide staircase swept down to the water. I swam to it and stood up on the first step, water dripping off me from the sea, water falling down on me from the sky.

This was the palace inside the storm that stole my life away. And the Ink King was its heart. Jimmy, who started all of this, who took what he wanted no matter who it hurt. I couldn't just let him do that. Not with *my* family.

The falling rain didn't scare me now. I knew what was real and what wasn't. I knew who was to blame, and this time I could stop him.

CHAPTER *21*

THE STEPS WERE EMPTY, AND I CLIMBED. EVEN THROUGH THE
falling rain, I could see where fire ripped the sky. It heated the
clouds and bathed the white marble palace in an angry hue.

I took the steps up until I stood on a wide landing in front of
an archway as tall and wide as a house. Water sluiced down both
sides, pouring out of the mouths of carved fish and rushing
alongside the steps.

I walked through the archway into an immense throne room.
Tall windows were set in the walls, letting in the red light. They

had all been opened, and rain fell onto the floor. There were seven pools, so deep they must have gone all the way down to the bottom of the sea. Each was cut in the shape of a different sea animal. One was unmistakably a Grumpalon. Another a Swisher-swasher. There was a sea horse. A turtle. A squid. And something that looked like a jellyfish. The last was some kind of hook-nosed creature with fins.

Perhaps that was how Ripple—or Vella—met with all of her subjects. Did each undersea kingdom have its own audience pool? Thinking about Ripple made my stomach clench, and I shoved the thought away.

In the center of the room was Jimmy. He sat curled upon the throne, high atop a steep incline of pink coral. He was a clot of black with his octopus pumping ink around him, a rotten spot on the Wishing World. And Ripple was just going to let him take over.

Jimmy jumped to his feet.

"I knew you'd cheat," he said. "Just like you did at the Starfield. Your friends cheated, too. They kept on fighting. Not supposed to do that. Not sure why the Robsombulous didn't suck them away. I'm sure you had something to do with that, too." He held up a hand. "Doesn't matter. We showed them."

"Where is Theron?"

"I taught the brat a lesson. I showed them all that I am king here. Not you or the stupid fish girl."

I wanted to thump him like a big Whac-A-Mole. I could write a giant mallet into existence. But I didn't. I tried to stay calm. "Give me my family, and I'll . . ." I faltered, thinking of Gruffy, Pip, and Squeak. I cleared my throat and pushed the thought away. "Give them to me, and I'll go. We don't need to fight."

He shook his head. "Gotta get every little thing you want, don't you? Couldn't just leave it alone. You're too selfish."

"It's my family!"

"So? Just because someone wants parents who love them doesn't mean they get them!" He flicked his hand at me. "You're not fair, Loreliar. Not a bit of you. You win, and you get what you want. You lose, and you still get what you want. But not me. You would think a father would want me to be happy, but no. My father only cares about what *he* wants. 'Take me to the Wishing World, son. Take me there and I'll get you an iPad.'" Jimmy clenched his teeth and his eyes blazed. "Well," he said. "He can keep his stupid iPad, and you can go home empty-handed."

"Give them back."

The ink pumped around him, deepening the shadows, framing him. "How did you describe the spelling bee at school? Oh yeah, '*The spelling bee where I lost.*'" He said it in a whiney voice, like that was supposed to be my voice or something.

"So what?"

"You came in nineteenth out of twenty. You were horrible," he continued as though I hadn't said anything. "And what did your parents do? Patted you on the head. Told you how great you were anyway. And you pouted and hugged them and mwah mwah mwah." He made exaggerated kissing noises. "Did you ever think about anyone else? Someone who might have won?"

"I don't care who won—"

"It was ME!" he shouted, and black billowed out far enough to touch the walls. "*Your* parents hugged you even though you stunk. You were the worst speller ever. Do you know what *my* dad did?"

"Jimmy—"

"NOTHING! He wasn't even there. No one told *me* good job. I got to take my ribbon home and throw it in the garbage. 'Take me to the Wishing World, Jimmy,' that's all my dad ever says." Jimmy clenched his fists, panting. Then he shook his head. "Well, he doesn't matter anymore. And neither do you."

He pointed his finger at the shadows by the base of the throne. The darkness peeled away, revealing a cage of black bars. My parents were lying inside. They seemed unharmed, except for the fact that they were pale and still, sleeping like vampires.

"It's about what I want now. They belong to me."

"Mom! Dad!" I ran forward.

"They're not leaving. But you are. Finally." Jimmy pointed at me.

A long shadow tentacle coiled around my leg from behind.

"You lose, Loreliar. Get it? You lose and I win. And this time it's going to matter!"

"Jimmy! Please! They're my parents—" I cried. The tentacle yanked me off my feet and pulled me toward the shadows.

"Not anymore. I'm not patting you on the head and giving you what you want. You can live my life and I'll live yours. You can have my dad." He laughed. "Take him! I hate him!"

"Jimmy!" I shouted.

"Go back to Earth!" He gestured again. I could feel the Wishing World shimmer around me, fading into a painting.

I saw a flicker of my basement in Jimmy's shadows. The tentacle dragged me closer.

No!

I ignored Jimmy and his craziness. I closed my eyes and imagined things the way I wanted them to be. I was staying here. I was staying until my family was safe.

I wrote one word on the air.

Stay.

Flames seared the inside of my ribs; I clenched my teeth.

I opened my eyes. The tentacle released my leg. The palace rumbled; the floor shook. Jimmy's portal faded.

"You have to go home!" Jimmy yelled. "This is my world!" His fists trembled. He stopped on the stairs, halfway between the throne and the floor.

"This place is for all children—"

"Not you!" he shouted. "It hates you so much the sky is ripping apart just to get rid of you. Your friend told me everything: how you tore open the Wishing World because you're so selfish. How you're killing it." The black cloud at the base of the throne pillar parted to reveal another cage. Sir Real slumped inside in his winged fox form. He wasn't moving. He didn't look like he was breathing.

"I found him sneaking," Jimmy said. "Looking for you. Looking to cheat." He stroked the octopus that hovered over him. "But we fixed him. Just like that stupid griffon."

"Where is Gruffy?"

"My Ratsharks finished him, and that stupid parrot, too."

"No!"

"This is my world! You don't get to have friends here!"

A mighty screech made me jump.

Gruffy swooped through the archway and landed like a cannonball. The marble popped under his claws, chips flying as he slid to a stop. His left wing drooped, and he had long scratches on his lion's flanks. He started up the stairs toward Jimmy. Squeak rode on the top of his head, and Pip flew in after them.

"Your Ratsharks are brutal," Gruffy said. He was limping. "But they have no heart. They were no match for the Mirror Man."

Darthorn strode through the archway. Water dripped from him, and his mirrors gleamed orange and red, reflecting the sky. His gaze fell on the cages at the base of the throne.

"Mom! Dad!" Darthorn's deep voice changed into Theron's. The mirrors slid aside, and he shrank to normal size. He sprinted toward their cage.

"No!" Jimmy shouted. A dozen ink tentacles slithered out from the giant ink cloud, catching Theron just as he reached Mom and Dad. The shadows formed another cage around him.

Theron growled and began to grow again, the mirrors sliding back into place. But the cage changed, becoming coils of black that bound him, just like they had bound Gruffy in the tunnel in Azure City. More ink pumped from the octopus until Theron was completely covered in black. He struggled and fell forward onto his face.

I hastily wrote on the air.

The Mirror Man broke free.

Jimmy grunted, and I felt his will push against mine like a flat stone on my forehead. I pushed harder.

A crack ran across the marble floor. The ground shook again like an earthquake.

Gruffy launched himself at Jimmy, but the octopus shot from Jimmy like a bullet and met Gruffy in midair. Shadow tentacles sprouted in every direction and grabbed Gruffy, slamming him against the wall. They vanished in a cloud of ink.

"Gruffy!"

Jimmy's concentration was broken. I turned back to Theron.

The Mirror Man, I wrote—

The world shook again, throwing me to my knees.

Gruffy lunged out of the black cloud. The octopus's tentacles were tight around his neck, squeezing. Gruffy bit again and again, but the bites had no effect. The octopus was choking him! The creature created another cloud of ink and they disappeared into it.

"Gruffy!" I shouted.

"He's dead," Jimmy said from right behind me, appearing out of the billowing ink at the base of the throne's pillar. "And so are you."

I spun, and he leapt at me, a knife raised in one hand.

Flower! I scrawled on the air.

Jimmy hit me in the chest with a tulip. The dagger was gone.

He growled, but before he could lash out again, a gigantic crack ran up the side of the throne. Half of the coral pedestal sheared off and fell toward us. Jimmy shouted and jumped out of the way just in time, slamming up against the pillar as the coral crashed right between us.

Coral takes Ink King, I wrote, and the words burned on the air. The coral at Jimmy's back leapt forward, enclosing his wrists and ankles in pink manacles.

Cracks raced in all directions away from me. The floor became a giant puzzle being pulled apart. The water in the shaped pools turned beet red. The ceiling sliced open and chunks fell. Red-tinted rain showered down all around us.

"The princess is here. The princess is here." Pip appeared, flapping toward me.

I looked up to see Ripple emerge from the farthest pool. She was blue again, not the lavender-eyed, pale-skinned Vella Wren.

She looked at me, and I thought she would suck me away from Jimmy's throne room, send me back to Earth or another part of Veloran.

Instead, she pointed at the octopus wrapped around Gruffy's head and a plume of water shot from the closest pool like it was a fire hose. It nailed the octopus in the head, spinning it away from Gruffy. The octopus regained its balance, started back. Ripple hit it with another blast, smashing it into the wall. The octopus fled then, flying out of one of the tall windows.

Gruffy lay at the base of the back wall. Unsteadily, he rose to his feet. He looked battered and broken. I stood up and looked to Theron and my caged parents. I started toward them.

"Squeak!"

I looked back and saw Squeak by the edge of Sir Real's cage.

"Squeak squeak!" he insisted.

Sir Real had awoken, and he was in his human form now. He held onto a shadow bar of his cage with one hand and gestured to me with the other. "Lorelei . . ." he murmured. "You must go . . ." His voice was so quiet I could barely hear him. "It is almost done. Veloran is almost gone."

"I'm not leaving them," I said. I took a step toward my parents' cage, writing on the air.

Vanish.

The strength of my story rippled out, but when it hit the cage, it lashed back, blowing like a hurricane and knocking me to the ground. It drove me and Sir Real's cage toward a crack where water sloshed up and almost took us over the edge. I fought the wave, grabbing at the uneven ground. I caught Squeak by the tail as he flowed past me. The water receded. I scrambled to my feet and put Squeak on safe ground.

Jimmy growled and thrashed against the coral shackles. "You're not getting them. You'll never get them!"

I clenched my fists, looked around helplessly. My gaze fell on Gruffy, lopsided, his wing hanging down.

"You will kill him," Sir Real said. "You will kill all of them."

"Gruffy wants me to stop Jimmy more than anyone!" I flung back at Sir Real.

"Because he was made for you. He was born to die for you," Sir Real said. "What are you willing to do for him?"

"Shut up!" I said to Sir Real.

"Will you kill him to get what you want?"

"It's not me! Jimmy is the . . ." I choked.

"Do not listen to the Flimflam, Doolivanti," Gruffy said sternly. "If you leave, you let this villain win. That injustice cannot be borne." He jumped over the chasm between us, landed badly, and his front leg buckled. He crashed to the cracked marble floor, then painstakingly stood up again. He shook his great eagle head. "Take your brother home. Regain your family and make things right."

"Do not listen," Sir Real said. "He is—"

"He's what?!" I whirled on Sir Real.

"He is what you want him to be!" Sir Real shouted. "You made him to protect you. To serve you. To fight for you! That is what he is. He cannot make the right decision, but you can." Sir Real looked at Squeak. "What about the mouse, *chica*? He is your wisdom. Remember? The little brilliant one. Are you listening to the mouse?"

"I can't understand him! I never could!"

"Please, Lorelei," Sir Real said.

I clenched my teeth and stared at my parents. Right there. Right in front of me. I could free them.

"You've created wonders while you have been here," Sir Real pleaded. "Do not destroy them. Do not—"

"Wonders? I haven't—"

"*Sí!* Wonders! I have marveled at you from the first moment. You did not let Veloran change you. You kept your own name. You did not use Veloran to escape. You used it to grow stronger. To grow up."

"I didn't—"

"All I ever did was hide," Sir Real said, his dark eyes haunted. "This is the choice we are all given the first moment we come here. To get what we want. And now, you have it. Your family is here, and you wish to be the child again and not make the hard choice. But these decisions are why you are brilliant. It is why you kept your own name. It is why Jimmy cannot beat you."

"You want me to *let* him beat me!"

"Do you not see how much larger you are? He is just a boy. And you . . ." He hesitated, bowed his head. "Do not make my mistake," he murmured. "I ran away. I did not stand up for who I am. I did not tell my father I am a painter and face the consequences. I did not ever become the person I could have been. And I did not understand how wrong I was until I met you. You are yourself no matter who tells you to be another. Don't you see? You are what Veloran can make all children." He slumped against the bars, as though the speech had spent his strength. "Do not do it," he whispered, so low it sounded like he was talking to himself. "Don't destroy this place for every other child who needs it."

I felt the strain pulling against me. Just standing here was hard now. The Wishing World was trying to push me out, and I was pitting my will against what Vella had called the "fabric of the painting." I looked over at Ripple, but she only stood there, as though she had never been Vella Wren, as though she was only my faithful companion the sea princess.

The ground rumbled again. The sky was beet red.

I could defeat Jimmy. He was finished. His inky octopus had fled. The Ratsharks were gone. I could rip open his cage.

"Squeak," Squeak said softly, and I looked down at the little mouse. His charcoal fur was wet, plastered against his tiny body. He looked scrawny, tiny next to Sir Real's cage, but his eyes glimmered.

I can't understand you, I thought. But I realized that was a lie. In this moment, I knew exactly what Squeak would say.

I looked at Gruffy. He was watching me, alert, ready to make the sacrifice. Pip hovered next to him and for once, the toucan had nothing to say.

The outer walls of the castle crumbled. Huge stones fell, cracking against the ground and splashing into the sea. The entire sky was the awful burning rip.

I screamed my frustration, turned to Jimmy, and grabbed his arm . . .

. . . and let go of the Wishing World.

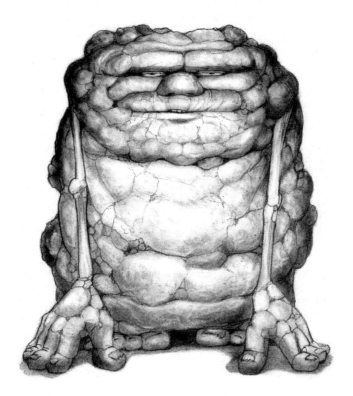

CHAPTER *22*

VELORAN WENT FLAT. GRUFFY, PIP, SQUEAK, RIPPLE, AND SIR
Real, bathed in red light, became characters in a painting
moving away from us. Blackness flooded around Jimmy and me,
washed us backward.

"No!" Jimmy shouted, his voice stretching long. "I'm the king
of the Wishing World!" He reached for my neck. I fought him,
gripping his wrists to stop him from strangling me. His fingers
groped desperately, hooking into my necklace. He twisted, and
the necklace snapped. We tumbled separately through the dark.

Shapes flickered overhead. Water pipes, heating vents and electrical wires. Cluttered shelves slowly appeared to my left. The many-armed furnace appeared to my right. It was my basement, and I was alone.

That cold realization swept through me, and I spun, looking around desperately.

Jimmy wasn't here.

I had grabbed him, pulled him with me. But he wasn't here. I climbed up on the shelves and looked back into the crawl space, all the way to the front of the house. Nothing.

He had been *with* me.

I clapped a hand to my throat. The necklace was gone, too. The comet stone. My key to Veloran. Gruffy's feather. All gone. Jimmy had yanked it off me.

"No!" My heart beat faster; I couldn't get enough air. I had failed at every single thing. I'd never see Theron again, never see Mom and Dad. I'd given them up, and now I had nothing. I had even less than when I'd gone to the Wishing World. Now I didn't even have hope.

I slumped against the crumbling brick wall, skidded to the ground, and hugged my knees. A sob shuddered through me. I was out of ideas. I was out of everything.

The door above opened and bright light spilled down the stairway. I squinted, trying to block the glare with my hand.

Mr. Schmindly's praying mantis silhouette hunched at the top, his hands together in front of himself. The lenses of his glasses glinted.

"Well, you certainly look a little more compliant. Are you ready to tell the truth now?" he asked, as though he'd just put me down here, as though I hadn't traveled the length of Veloran, found my family, and fought Jimmy in a crumbling palace beneath a red sky.

"Let me out," I said weakly. It didn't sound like I meant it, even to me. Did it matter if I stayed down here forever? Would any place in the world be any brighter?

Mr. Schmindly smiled thinly, leaned even farther down. "Let me in," he whispered. "Show me the doorway, Lorelei, and you can go home."

Home.

"You can't give me my home," I said. "And I'll never let you into the Wishing World. Never."

Mr. Schmindly's mouth turned down in a frown. "You will," he said menacingly. "Or you'll live the rest of your life down here—"

There was a sound like running feet and something small slammed into Mr. Schmindly like a ram. He flew from view, crying out as he crashed into my bedroom to the right. Then there was another crashing noise, like a dresser had fallen on him.

I gasped and stood up.

Theron appeared in the doorway, fists clenched at his sides and his lips pressed together firmly. He glared in the direction he had bulldozed Mr. Schmindly.

"THERON!" I leapt to my feet and raced up the stairs. I threw my arms around him. "How . . . ? How . . . ?"

Distracted, he pushed me away, his fierce gaze still on Mr. Schmindly, who was sprawled on the floor, an old chair tangled in his legs. The glasses had fallen off his face, and he groped around for them. Theron pointed at him, his brows knitted together. "You get up and you'll be sorry."

"Theron! How?" I stammered.

He finally looked at me and grinned. "Hi, Lore."

"How did you get back?"

"Oh. Him." Theron stuck a thumb over his shoulder in the other direction. Inside our back door stood Sir Real in his human form, his wavy black hair tumbling down over his face. He was stooped and panting, as though he had run a marathon, and he leaned heavily on the door's handle.

"Sir Real!"

He gave me a wan smile. "André," he said softly. "My real name is André."

I went to him in a daze. "But, you said if you told me your real name—"

"That I would have to come back to Earth. I know." He laughed, his voice tired. "But you saved my Flimflams. You saved the Wishing World for all the other children. I could not stay. Not when I could give you what you most wanted."

"What I most . . ." I spun around.

Standing by the sink in the kitchen, blinking and looking completely confused, were my parents.

"No way!" I launched myself toward them. Mom and Dad barely had time to look up before I slammed into them. I wrapped an arm around each of them and didn't let go. I was never going to let them go again.

"Hey there, Lori-Bee," Dad said.

"Jelly sandwich," Mom said.

"And I'm the jelly," I said, crying, burying my head in Mom's shoulder. "I'm the jelly in the middle . . ."

CHAPTER 23

I SAT IN THE BASEMENT OF AUNTIE CARRIE AND UNCLE JONE'S house with Theron. Their basement was a totally different kind than the one in our house. The walls were painted, for starters. And there were short, wide windows high up, next to the ceiling, which was white stucco with a fancy overhead light. And there was also carpet, cool and soft. Theron and I sat cross-legged, facing each other.

There had been a great deal of confusion about our return

from Veloran. First thing I did after hugging my parents for an eternity was to ask Theron how he and André had gotten back.

"It's actually been a while since you left, at least in the Wishing World," Theron had said. "The cage around Mom and Dad sorta melted away. The storm blew itself out and all the Beetlins and Ratsharks took off once Jimmy was gone. Anyway, we spent some days helping Ripple put her palace back together while André's Flimflams chased down the octopus Jimmy was using to go between worlds. Took them a while, but they painted a harness right on the thing. Made it take us back here."

"Jimmy didn't come back to Veloran?"

"I thought he was here," Theron had said.

I told Theron of my disappointment in losing Jimmy. He could be anywhere, and that made me more than a little nervous.

But there were other concerns that caught up with us about then, and I didn't get to chase the thought.

The police had showed up, responding to a phone call made by Auntie Carrie, who was looking for me and told them to check my house first. The police had a list of questions; they wanted explanations, and there were no answers that satisfied them. None that adults would believe, anyway. My parents had reappeared after a year. My brother had, too. And of course there was André, who lied and told the police he had no parents at all. That not only baffled the police, it baffled me until André told me the truth: he had been in the Wishing World for almost a century. His parents had died a long time ago. Theron and I begged Mom and Dad to let him stay with us and they said yes, and the police had allowed it.

But my parents didn't remember anything about the Wishing World or the last year. The police questioned them for days, bringing in psychologists and other experts to try to get the truth. They also questioned Theron, who happily told them everything.

Except no one could hang onto the stories. Even right after Theron told them something, the police would get strange looks on their faces, then begin asking the same questions. Theron finally yelled at them to stop talking.

I didn't say much about Veloran, but I gave them everything about Mr. Schmindly. From him tripping me in the dining room to throwing me down the basement stairs to locking me in. I showed them the finger marks on my arms, the scrapes on my elbows and chin.

The police's attention had turned to Mr. Schmindly then. Had he locked us all down there? A psychiatrist could prescribe drugs. Had he given the whole group of us drugs that fogged our memories? And why did his daughter, Tabitha, have a split lip and a black eye? Apparently, when we came back from Veloran, she was up the street at Walgreens getting a cold pack for her face. She had returned to flashing police lights and had tried to run. They caught her.

Also, apparently, Jimmy had been missing for a year. All the proper missing child reports had been filed, but now there was a heap-load of doubt on Mr. Schmindly. What had he done with his son?

In a flash, it was Mr. Schmindly's turn to answer a lot of questions. And the answers he stammered out kinda sucked. The police seemed to feel the same way, and they took him to jail.

The police let Mom and Dad join Theron, André, and me at Auntie Carrie and Uncle Jone's house when they realized that they honestly had no recollection, and we had all stayed here for the last day and a half, trying to sort through the last year. My family was together again. That was what mattered, and I was never letting them out of my sight again.

Of course, I told Mom and Dad the whole truth, but it didn't work with them any more than it had with the police. There was something about the Wishing World that wouldn't stick in the minds of adults. I thought at least Dad would believe. With his excitement about Narolev's Comet, the camping trip, and making the comet stone charms for us, I thought maybe he already knew about Veloran somehow. But a few minutes after Theron and I would tell him the story, he'd ask again what happened. It made me wonder how Mr. Schmindly knew that there was a Wishing World at all. Had he gone there as a child and returned, like all of us? Was that what let him remember? Were there other adults who knew about the Wishing World?

"They're not going to believe," Theron had finally said to me. "They're grown-ups."

I wondered if, when I got older, I wouldn't be able to remember Veloran anymore. André said I had grown up in the Wishing World. Did that mean I would forget? Narolev's Comet had finally left the night sky, and the Wishing World seemed so far away, a bright and magical place. Details about Gruffy, Pip, Squeak, and Ripple faded a little more every day.

It hurt my heart to think that they might vanish altogether. What if soon I couldn't recall Pip's blue plumage? Or Gruffy's fierce and lovable face? I thought about writing myself into the

Wishing World again, trying to go back, but I didn't dare. I had done so much damage. And I didn't even know if it was possible, now that I had no comet stone.

"It might happen to us, too, you know," I said to Theron, and I sighed. "The more time that goes by, the less I believe it. Even André is starting to seem like a boy we already knew."

"Yeah?" Theron said. He had asked me to come to the basement while the adults were busy, and he had an impish grin on his face.

"Why are you smiling?"

He had Auntie Carrie's hand mirror, stolen from the bathroom. He wasn't supposed to take anything from Auntie Carrie's bathroom, but Theron often "forgot" rules. He put it on the carpet, reached behind his back, and pulled out my necklace with the comet stone. The long, white griffon feather dangled from it.

"Theron!" I gasped.

"You dropped this."

I hugged him. Then I punched him in the shoulder.

"Ow!"

"Why didn't you give this to me before?" I demanded.

He laughed, rubbing his arm. "The police took it from André. Evidence or something, but they gave it back today."

"Where'd he get it?"

"Go ask him. Be sure to punch him, too."

I pressed the feather against my cheek, then held it up and looked at it for a long time. I brought it to my mouth and whispered. "I'll never forget. Never ever."

Theron grinned, then picked up the mirror again. He held his silver stone knight in his other hand.

"What?" I asked. "What is it?"

He held the mirror up to me, squinching his eyes in concentration.

I looked at my own reflection, then suddenly I was looking at a different face.

"Doolivanti?" Gruffy said.